UNFAMOUS MEN

UNFAMOUS MEN

a novel

JEFF GOMEZ

HARROW

Harrow Books

To Luis Gonzales Gomez
(1909–1995)

*This is a story of misfortune. Or so it would seem.
The end is not yet told.*

—Cormac McCarthy, *The Crossing*

THE CAR STOPPED at the edge of Saticoy. Two men got out. The first was short and dark-skinned, with high cheekbones and eyes so brown they looked black. He hopped quickly out of the passenger side of the front seat, a brown paper bag under his arm. He stepped onto the running board before hitting the road. The second man had lighter skin and was nearly double the size of his friend. He took up most of the back seat of the beat-up, navy-blue '36 Plymouth. The car tilted when he got out. The smaller man thanked the driver and watched as the car continued to its destination.

The two men turned to face the small town. It held a church, hardware store, post office, bank, three grocery stores, and four bars. A set of train tracks led to a small wooden depot and platform. Side streets were dotted with small one- and two-bedroom houses, some of them not more than shacks. In the backyards were cheaply built lean-tos for boarders, Mexicans who worked in the fields. In front of a row of Quonset huts built at the start of the war, an elderly woman swept dust off the hard-packed dirt of her front yard. Telephone poles placed around the town made a cat's cradle of wires above the buildings. Black power lines stretched down to each house and business. Shiny new TV antennas reflected the late-afternoon sun.

The larger man looked up, as if finally realizing that he was no longer inside the car. His head was nearly shaven, which, when he stood up straight, made him look like a missile. He pointed toward the town. But the smaller man, who had jet-black hair combed straight back, shook his head and began to walk in the opposite direction, toward the Santa Clara River. The larger man followed.

He stared at the ground as he walked, eyes down and chin placed firmly on his chest. His arms were raised slightly, his huge hands joined and suspended in front of his belly, fingers interlocked. His steps were short, despite his long legs. The smaller man, his own legs slightly bowed, moved with a nervous bounce. His arms held the paper bag close to his side, as if he were afraid someone was going to come by and take it, even though the streets were empty.

Their clothes were ordinary and mostly clean. Jeans, white shirts, denim jackets, and black boots turned brown from walking through the lettuce field that morning. They were without luggage, and except for the brown bag held by the smaller man, they had no possessions of any kind. They didn't even have hats, even though it'd been a hot day, unseasonably warm for March in California.

As the two men hiked down to the water's edge, sycamores and live oaks gave shade to sagebrush and cactus. The sandy, gravelly riverbed was visible through the clear, running water. Further downstream, willow and poplar trees could be seen beyond a row of low shrubbery, the river winding toward where it emptied into the sea near the harbor in Ventura.

The men entered a clearing that had a large expanse of blond sand surrounded by a ring of pepper trees. As they stood there, the smaller man barked, "Well, Juanito, you might as well sit down. This is going to be our bed for the night."

The larger man lowered himself onto the bank of the river. Sand pushed out all around him. The smaller man at first only squatted, restless, not wanting to commit. But he, too—without any other real option—finally sat down with a huff. He placed the brown paper bag near a bush and began picking up pebbles, throwing them expertly into the water. For a few minutes, the splash of the skipping stones was the only sound.

"Tomás?" The larger man's voice was small and childlike. His face, with rolls of fat at his neck, along with a large forehead made him look like a giant infant. Only the stubble on his chin and the sideburns hanging below his short hair gave any hint as to his real age. "I'm *hungry.*"

Tomás didn't reply. He just kept on picking up pebbles and throwing them into the river. He tried to force Juanito's presence, as well as their current situation, out of his mind. He focused instead on the rushing water. He thought back to his days in the US Navy. He'd spent as much time as possible looking over the deck of his cruiser, staring down at the churning water and imagining the worlds that lived in the depths beneath the surface.

"Tomás?" Juanito repeated.

"Look, I know you're hungry," he snapped. "I'm hungry, too. How could I not be? We haven't eaten since breakfast." Tomás looked at the darkening sky. "And all we've got for dinner is what that guy just gave us. But I'm warning you, it's not going to be much."

Juanito looked around, examining his surroundings. He touched the sand, as if to make sure it was real. He then looked over his shoulder, at the path that had led them from the road to the river.

"Why didn't we get anything to eat in town?"

"I told you before, Juanito," said Tomás, his voice scolding, "we don't have any money."

Juanito considered this. It always took a long time for his thoughts to form. "What happened to the money my aunt left me?"

Tomás replied, his voice full of innocence, "What are you talking about?"

"They gave it to you because I couldn't be trusted." A breeze momentarily distracted Juanito as he looked from tree to tree to see the waving of the branches. When the wind stopped, his thought was almost gone with it. He was about to ask again about food when he remembered. "The money, Tomás. They gave it to you. For me. For both of us. So we could go see my uncle in Los Angeles. That's what we're doing, right?"

Before answering, Tomás took something out of his jacket pocket and played with it in his hand, nervously. "That was the plan, yes."

"So, what happened? Why aren't we there?"

"We got . . . sidetracked," Tomás answered, reluctantly. "But we'll get there, don't you worry."

Juanito turned toward the town and clutched his stomach. "I'm hungry, Tomás. I need something to eat."

"I can give you what we have now, Juanito. But once it's gone, it's gone." Tomás looked through the canopy of trees to the sky, trying to judge how long it'd be before it was completely dark. "We might as well save it for a bit. Try to make it last."

Juanito thought about this for a few seconds. He had another thought about the food, but it escaped and was replaced by another. "We left before getting paid."

"What?" Tomás said. "You know I can't hear you when you put your chin in your chest like that."

"Our jobs," Juanito answered, looking up slightly. "That ranch. Picking lettuce. We left before getting paid. Why?"

At first, Tomás didn't answer. But then he turned quickly and snapped, "You want to pick lettuce for the rest of your life?"

"I want to be with my uncle."

"I know, Juanito. I know."

"I could be in bed right now, instead of sitting here on this sand. I could have had pie and cake and all kinds of good things for dinner. Instead, I'm out here in the cold with you."

"Well, if you don't like it, then maybe you should leave. Go out on your own, if you think you can make it to Los Angeles by yourself." Tomás pointed back toward the town. "Hell, leave right now. Maybe you can hitch a ride and be there by midnight."

Juanito raised his head and looked toward Saticoy. "You don't think I could do it, but I could." Juanito tried to make his voice sound firm, but it wavered and was hardly above a whisper. His eyes were practically closed. "And I should have, too. I'd have been there by now."

"You think so?" Tomás began to laugh. "You'd have gotten on the wrong bus and ended up in Canada, you big fool. Or wound up dead in a ditch."

Juanito blinked. He didn't know where Canada was, but figured maybe it was near Los Angeles and that might be close enough.

"Of course, if you did go," Tomás said, sounding sinister, "you'd have to explain what happened to all of his sister's money you were supposed to bring him."

Juanito's doughy face became gripped with fear. "But I don't have any of that money. You were in charge of it, and you lost it."

"And that's what I keep telling you." Tomás motioned to the trees and orchards and fields all around them. "That's why we're here. To work for a couple of weeks and earn it back. And then we can go to your uncle's in Los Angeles. Okay?"

This seemed to satisfy Juanito. After he answered, "Okay," his face fell back into its normal shape, his chin returning to its usual place on his chest.

Tomás turned and began playing with whatever was in his hand. The small clicking noise attracted the attention of Juanito, who leaned over to see what it was.

"What have you got there, Tomás, a toy?" He moved even closer. "I'd like a toy."

"It's nothing. Mind your own business."

Tomás tried to turn so that Juanito couldn't see what was in his hand, but Juanito reached out and grabbed Tomás by the shoulder. When he pulled, Juanito tossed Tomás like a rag doll. A pair of red dice with white spots fell onto the sand, making two small indentations on the shore. Juanito gasped as he reached down to pick them up. They looked like ladybugs in his huge palm.

"You told me you had gotten rid of these."

Tomás raised himself from the riverbank and grinned. "Yeah, well, I meant to."

Juanito continued to stare at the dice, giving them a dirty look. As if they were the root of all their troubles.

"You and your gambling, and girls. I'm tired of it." He raised his arm and threw the dice into the bushes.

The grin on Tomás's face quickly disappeared. He began to frantically look through the brush. "You didn't have to do that," he called over his shoulder. "I'd have laid off them."

As Tomás grumbled to himself and continued to rummage through the bushes, looking for the dice, Juanito pulled his knees into his body and wrapped his arms around his legs. He began to rock back and forth, digging himself deeper into the sand with each motion.

"You told me you were done with those dice. You told me you'd already thrown them away."

Tomás gave up on finding them and returned to the riverbank. He sat down. "I know, Juanito, and I'm sorry. I meant to. I just hadn't gotten around to it yet. But I would have, honest."

"You lie, Tomás. You told me a lie in Hollister, too. That's why we had to go and pick that lettuce. You gambled the money away before we even left. That's why we had to work. It wasn't me. It was you."

Tomás began to defend himself, but stopped. He knew Juanito would soon forget what he was mad about and the whole thing would blow over. It always did. So he just kept quiet.

The two of them sat there, just listening to the wind and watching the trees and bushes turn dark brown as the sun continued to set. Tomás reached for more pebbles, but when he threw them into the river, he couldn't see where they entered the water. He only heard the hollow splash and gulp as the stones disappeared under the surface.

Juanito finally spoke. "Where are we, Tomás?"

"Jesus, Juanito, you forgot that already? We're in Saticoy. Tomorrow we're going to a ranch I heard about when I was working at Limoneira in Santa Paula, right after the war." Tomás tried to look in the direction of the ranch, but all he could see were trees. "It's not far from here. They always need a few extra guys, so we should be able to get some work."

"What are we going to do there, Tomás?"

"Pick lemons, you big baby. But not for long. I figure once we get just a few paychecks, we'll have earned back your aunt's money. Then we can go to Los Angeles and see your uncle. Okay?"

"I miss my aunt."

"I know, Juanito."

"And I miss Hollister."

"I miss it, too." But for Tomás, this was a lie. He had nothing in Hollister anymore except a few cousins who barely remembered him. He'd never known his mom, and his dad had died while he was in the Pacific.

"I'm hungry, Tomás. Can we eat now?"

Tomás nodded and retrieved the crumpled paper bag from the riverbank. It felt lighter than he remembered. He knew it wouldn't be enough to feed them both, let alone Juanito. He reached in and pulled out the various bundles of wax paper. He unwrapped them to discover a few lumps of pork, a dried heap of beans and three tortillas. He placed the food on top of the bag, and set the bag on the sand between himself and Juanito.

Juanito lunged at the food. Tomás ripped a tortilla in half and scooped up some beans and meat.

"The pork's a little sour," he said. "And the tortillas are like leather. No way was this his supper for today, like he told us. At least, if it was, it wasn't fresh this morning."

Juanito, noisily chewing and swallowing, didn't pay any attention to Tomás. He just kept on eating.

In a few minutes, there was nothing left but the bag and wax paper.

Juanito, licking his lips, looked toward the river.

"I know what you're thinking," Tomás said. He stuffed

the bits of wax paper back into the bag, crumpled it up, and threw it against a bush. "You can probably drink it."

Like a bear, Juanito walked on his hands and knees and then lowered his head into the water. He took half a dozen gulps, his body rising and falling rhythmically. When he returned to the riverbank, the bottom half of his massive face was wet and the collars of his jacket and shirt were dotted with splashes of water.

"Feel better?" Tomás asked.

"I'm still hungry. I want more."

Juanito spoke as if Tomás had the power to produce food out of thin air. As if, just by asking for another meal, one would magically appear.

"Tomorrow, Juanito. Tomorrow." Tomás turned and looked at his friend, but Juanito didn't raise his head or make eye contact. "We'll get three meals a day at the new place. Meals better than that one, I promise you."

"I don't like working in the fields, Tomás."

"Neither do I, but it's the only thing we can get hired to do. You think that if they won't let us eat in their restaurants or use their bathrooms, that we can get a job in an office, or even a garage? No, the fields are our only choice."

"Not in Los Angeles. Not at my uncle's."

Tomás's face lit up. He stood and looked back at Saticoy. "You're right, Juanito. Most of the guys over there have got only one thing ahead of them for the rest of their lives. Stoop labor. Breaking their backs for pennies. Drifting from crop to crop and ranch to ranch. Picking lemons or walnuts and living in the shadows.”

“But not us, Tomás.” Juanito raised his head and pointed at his chest with a thumb. For the first time that day, his big brown eyes were shining. “We’re different. Tell me again how it’s going to be for us.”

“We’re going to have a real home, Juanito. A place where we can live, and have stuff. A radio, and maybe even a TV. That’s all we want. A home. We don’t want no land.” Tomás kicked at the ground. “We just want to belong.”

Juanito nodded and continued to point at himself.

“We want to walk down the street without being stared at. Stay in one place, and not have to move around all the time. Be considered a part of this country, and not a foreigner.” Tomás’s voice turned soft and pleading, as if he were asking himself whether he was asking for too much. “Get paid the same as someone whose skin is a different color. And if you get hurt, you don’t lose your job.”

Juanito, still nodding, added, “And if we don’t want to work in the fields, why, then we won’t.”

“Exactly, Juanito. We’ll be able to choose any sort of work we want. Hell, the war’s been over for three years and I still don’t have a better job than when I left. Land of opportunity,” he scoffed. “I tell you, once they point you towards the fields and give you the short-handled hoe, they're never going to give you anything else."

"But not us," Juanito said.

"Not us," Tomás repeated.

Satisfied, Juanito stopped nodding. His head fell and his chin returned to his chest. Tomás sat back down and watched twigs and leaves slowly drift downstream.

"Listen, for tomorrow, at the ranch," Tomás said, "I want to teach you a few things."

"Teach me what, Tomás?" Juanito's face, happy just a few moments ago, turned sad. His chin dug into his chest even more than usual. "I'm not a good learner. I never made it past the third grade, you know that."

"Yeah, Juanito," Tomás said, "I know that. But if we're going to earn a little money, I need them to think you know what you're doing."

Tomás approached Juanito and grabbed an arm. He tried to lift him, but Juanito was like a rock and Tomás couldn't move him at all. He backed off and pleaded with his eyes. When Juanito finally stood up, Tomás noticed the crater of sand that'd been created in the riverbank.

"First of all," Tomás said as he looked Juanito up and down, "you're standing up too straight."

"But my aunt always told me—"

"I know what she told you, Juanito, but you need to forget all that now."

Tomás reached out and put his hands on Juanito's

back. To do so, he had to stand on the balls of his feet. Though Juanito looked big and doughy, his back was firm and made of muscle. Tomás placed his palm between Juanito's shoulder blades and pushed. Juanito slowly started to hunch over.

"Why do I have to do this, Tomás?"

"Because all the ranchers are white, and if you stand up too straight, it shows you can think for yourself. And the last thing they want, from someone who looks like us anyway, is a guy who can think for himself."

Tomás backed up and examined Juanito. He whispered to himself, "I'd tell you to look dumb, but you do an awfully good job of that already."

"What did you say, Tomás?"

"Nothing. Now, I need to dirty up your clothes."

"But they'll get dirty tonight."

"They need to be even dirtier. You need to look like a worker."

"I am a worker, Tomás. Remember the lettuce?"

"Yes, Juanito, we spent eight days picking lettuce up north. How could I possibly forget?"

Tomás closed his eyes and saw the logo, GARDEN BRAND PRODUCE, along with wooden crates and their colorful labels featuring a colony of rabbits frolicking in a vegetable patch.

"But that was yesterday." Tomás walked into the bushes and grabbed handfuls of dirt from where gnarled roots disappeared into the soft ground. He returned to Juanito and began rubbing the soil into the front of his friend's jacket. "These are your nice clothes, and you haven't worked a day in them."

"Why do we have to do this, Tomás?"

"You can't be well dressed, or appear intelligent. That's what they look for. When they see a guy like that, they figure he's trouble because he has a lot of big ideas. They don't want any big ideas."

"I don't know what big ideas are, Tomás."

As he kneeled down for more dirt, Tomás said over his shoulder, "Then I guess you're going to fit in just fine."

He tried to rub the dirt onto Juanito's shoulder, but couldn't reach. He handed the clumps of dirt to his friend so he could do it himself.

As Juanito rubbed the rocks and soil all over his clothes, as if each clod were a bar of soap on his body, he asked, "Why did we leave that other place, Tomás?"

Even though he knew what Juanito was talking about, Tomás responded, "What other place?"

"The lettuce. Goleta. Where we were this morning."

"Let's just say me and the boss didn't see eye to eye."

Juanito paused for a second as he tried to organize his thoughts. His memories were often like pieces of a puzzle that he just couldn't put together to make a picture. Finally, something clicked.

"It wasn't the boss, Tomás. It was that girl."

Tomás ignored him and turned again to the ground, this time to collect a number of large rocks. He barked, "Now, put out your hands."

Juanito dropped the dirt and put out his hands.

"Rub these rocks all over your hands. If you can, give yourself a blister or some cuts."

He did what he was told, wincing once or twice as the sharp edges of a rock broke his skin.

"My god." Tomás laughed. "A big guy like you, crying like a baby."

Juanito did this until his hands were dirtied and bruised. Tomás stepped back and examined his friend. Juanito looked suitably shabby.

"Okay, one last thing. They might ask you some questions."

Juanito tensed up. "What kind of questions?"

"It'll just be something basic like 'Have you ever picked before?' You just nod and say, 'Yes, I know what I'm doing.'"

"But that's a lie, Tomás."

He was going to try and reason with Juanito, telling him how not all lies are equal and that—in the grand scheme of things—this was a small lie, but he'd tried to explain things like that in the past and always came away frustrated. "I know it's a lie, Juanito, but you just say it, okay?"

Juanito nodded, uncertainly.

"Finally, when you're around those ranchers, you just speak Spanish like I'm talking to you now."

"We always speak Spanish to each other, Tomás."

"I know, but they might address you in English, and if they do, I want you to act like you don't understand."

Juanito looked puzzled. "Why? I speak English just fine—my aunt made sure I did. Almost got into the good school when I was a kid."

"Yeah, and what happened? They figured out how smart you wasn't?"

"No." Juanito's face clouded. "That wasn't until later."

"Then what was it?"

"They figured out I was a Mexican."

"What, the name Juan wasn't a clue?" Tomás looked down at his small hands and the dark brown skin of his arms, then he glanced over at Juanito. "Your aunt must have tried to pass you off as John. But she couldn't do anything about your last name being Sanchez."

There was silence for a moment as they both just stood there. Voices from town were carried on the breeze to the riverbank, only the sounds were too faint to be made out as words. The noise just mingled with the rustling of the pepper trees.

Juanito suddenly remembered what they'd been discussing. "Okay, Tomás. I won't speak English, I promise."

"That's a good boy, Juanito." Tomás patted his friend

on the elbow. "Besides, sometimes you can use it to your advantage."

"How?"

"Like, if they think you don't understand what they're saying, they'll talk about you. About how they're going to cheat you out of your wages or something. Then you can make sure that doesn't happen."

"But what if something slips out? If they ask me something in English, I'm not smart enough not to answer."

Tomás thought about this. "Well, if you don't think you can help yourself, then I guess there's nothing we can do."

There was silence again, except for a car honking somewhere near the train station.

"Money," Juanito finally said. "At the ranch, I mean. What do I say if they ask about money?"

Tomás kicked at the dirt. "For work like this, Juanito, they won't mention money. If we're lucky enough to get hired, then that's about all the luck we're going to get." He looked around. Toward the river, the bushes, the purple sky where stars were beginning to appear. "We'll get paid what they're paying, and we're not going to complain."

Juanito nodded his head like he understood, and his mouth began to form words, but instead of speaking he just flapped his arms up and down. While Juanito was doing that, Tomás began clearing away branches and leaves, creating a place where they could sleep.

The sun was now all the way down. The wind that blew through the trees had a chill. Settling into the cold sand, Tomás missed the bunkhouse back in Goleta. He felt foolish for having to leave the job the way they did. He was also beginning to regret his plan to not go to the lemon ranch until morning. He should have listened to Juanito and had the car from before drop them off right outside the bunkhouse instead of in Saticoy. The driver knew the ranch, said it'd be no problem. But it was too late to worry about that now.

"You might as well begin to settle in, Juanito. It's been a long enough day already, and you'll need your sleep for tomorrow."

Juanito nodded and stopped flapping his arms. He sat down and stretched out on the sand, looking like a beached whale. Tomás buttoned his jacket up all the way to his throat and tried to get comfortable.

The moon reflected on the river. All around them was the sound of the wind in the trees. In town, the last of the trucks returned from the fields, depositing the men back onto the street corners where they'd been picked up at dawn. Some of the men walked straight into a bar, spending the money they'd earned that day but hadn't yet been given. Others went to the market to buy food for families who were waiting for them.

"You asleep yet, Tomás?"

He yawned and put a hand in his pocket to feel for the dice, but they were gone. Tomás shrugged and figured it was better this way. They'd only ever brought him bad luck.

"Not yet, Juanito. Almost. You go to sleep."

"I will, Tomás. I just wanted to make sure about my uncle's. That we're headed to Los Angeles."

"Yes, Juanito, after the ranch. After we get some money. Then we'll go to your uncle's." Tomás yawned again. Once it passed, he closed his eyes and continued. "We'll finally stop running. We'll get far away from here. It won't be long now."

TOMÁS WOKE WITH the gray light of dawn after tossing and turning all night. He would have sworn he didn't sleep at all except he half remembered a dream about his father, so he figured he must have dozed off at one point. Juanito had slept like a bear, snoring for hours after falling asleep immediately. Tomás hadn't minded the snoring. That sound, along with the rushing of the river, nearly drowned out the noise that carried over from town of bottles smashing, horns honking, and men laughing or crying as they stumbled home from the bars. Just after dawn, flatbed trucks rolled in and picked up half the population of Saticoy from street corners. Tomás just sat there, staring at the river and waiting for his friend to wake up.

He knew breakfast was being served at the ranch. He also knew, if they waited too long, any jobs that might be available would get taken by someone else. There were always men around to work the fields, and Tomás became increasingly anxious as the minutes and hours passed. Not that he was eager to get into the fields. He didn't care much for the work, but it was something. And without it, he didn't know where else to go.

When it looked as if they might miss lunch, too, Juanito finally stirred.

Yawning, he sat up, looked around, and asked Tomás where they were. Instead of answering, Tomás stood up and reversed the course they'd come the night before, walking away from the river back toward town.

"Tomás," Juanito called out, "wait for me!"

Blinking and with sand sticking to half of his huge face, he scrambled to follow.

They walked past the town and turned down a road that was lined on either side with orchards. Telephone poles ran along one side of the road, the blacktop turned brown with dirt. A truck, with dozens of men in the back, passed them as they walked. The truck and the men were also covered in dirt. Tomás shielded his eyes from the sun and tried to see if the truck belonged to the ranch they were headed to, but he couldn't get a good look because of the glare.

Every two hundred yards or so, the row after row of lemon trees were broken up by lines of tall eucalyptus trees. These were windbreaks to keep the fruit from freezing. Windmills, which circulated air on cold nights, also dotted the orchards. The only thing that grew higher than the eucalyptus trees were the palm trees. Every ranch had them lining the long driveways that led to opulent houses where the growers lived. Red barns were also scattered amid the fields, peeking up here and there over the tops of the fruit trees.

After a half hour of walking, Tomás stopped and pointed to where a line of palm trees grew so high they were bending and swaying in the breeze, their trunks touching and even crossing.

"That's where we're going."

Juanito grunted.

They finally turned off the road and onto a wide dirt path deeply rutted from the dozens of trips a day the trucks made carrying men and lemons back and forth. At the end of the path was a house. It was large and Victorian, with a wraparound porch and dozens of ornate wooden details. Shutters, fences, screen doors, all painted in an array of colors. Juanito didn't notice the house, but when Tomás saw it, he whistled.

Juanito started to walk down the long driveway that led to the house. Tomás reached out to stop him.

"Not there, Juanito. That's where the owner lives. He won't want anything to do with us. We need to find the field boss, or his assistant."

They turned away from the driveway and walked along a dirt path that held a number of buildings.

As they passed a packing shed, a big building with a tin roof and corrugated tin walls, they could hear the churning and clanking of all the machinery inside. They could also hear women's voices speaking and joking in Spanish.

Just past the packing shed they came across a man working on a car, an old Chevy coupe from before the war. The huge hood was up, and the man was half inside it. It looked as if the car were eating him. Tomás, not able to see the man's face, called out in English. When the man pulled his head out, they saw that he was an old Mexican. He was short and had a bushy white mustache; the deep tan on his already-brown skin gave his face the appearance of leather. When Tomás spoke again, it was in Spanish. "Hello there, friend. We were hoping to get some work."

The man pushed up the brim of a floppy hat with a crescent wrench stained with grease. "I think the crews are already out for the day." His voice matched his face, tired and weathered. "But we can always use help."

He turned and shouted. Off the main dirt road was a path that led to half a dozen bunkhouses. From out of the first one came a young man. He was short and dark, even darker than Tomás. He walked slowly and stiffly, keeping the weight off his left foot with a homemade crutch made from an old push broom. He approached the trio as if in slow motion.

"Custodio," the old man said, "these two would like some work."

The young man, who couldn't have been more than

twenty, looked over Tomás and Juanito. Tomás looked like pretty much every other guy on the ranch, but he'd never seen anyone as big as Juanito. "You're in luck," he said. His teeth were big and white. "We had two run off this morning." He planted his crutch firmly in the dusty ground so he could scratch his chin. "Maybe I could get a message to Santos. He's the foreman. That would get you out there by lunch."

At the mention of food, Juanito finally looked up. Custodio smiled and began to lead the new men toward the bunkhouses.

The buildings were whitewashed adobe, with skinny doors of unpainted wood. They were low and squat, with just one small window to the side of the door. The roofs of wooden planks were slightly pitched. No two roofs matched. Where one sloped, another rose.

Custodio opened the door to the first one and walked in with some difficulty. Tomás and Juanito followed, Juanito having to bend at the waist to enter.

In the long room were six beds, three on each side. The bed frames were old and iron, topped with a thin mattress and sheets that were stained and had holes. Underneath each bed was a wooden crate. Four of them were filled with the belongings of men who were currently out in the orchards, while two were empty. The crates were filled mostly with clothes. Boots, denim jackets, work shirts. Out of one poked a Bible, in another was a radio, and one held a black-and-white photograph of an unsmiling woman with three small children. The room was lit by a bare light bulb hanging from the middle of the ceiling. The walls held no insulation against the cool, and there was no fan for relief from the heat.

Other than the beds, the only furniture in the room was a square wooden table near the back wall. Sitting around it were four wooden chairs, all of them mismatched in design and color. Two were unpainted while another was black and yet another—one that tilted, like the room itself, to one side—was white. On the wall above the table was tacked a cheaply printed poster of the Virgin of Guadalupe. Tómas saw it and grinned. He'd been looking at that image all his life.

Custodio pointed with his crutch. "These two bunks will be yours."

Tomás approached and sat down on one of the beds. He wondered about asking Custodio why the other two men left, but thought better of it. The stories of why men came and left the fields were the same as the fields themselves. All different yet similar. Besides, if he asked it would invite Custodio to ask about him and Juanito, and Tomás didn't want to answer any of those questions.

Juanito sat down on his bunk, the wire mesh creaking and nearly giving way. When he lay down and stretched out, his feet hung over the end of the bed frame by more than a foot and the mattress sank so low, it almost touched the floor. But it was better than the riverbank, so he smiled as he turned one way and then another.

He spotted a stack of comic books poking out of the crate underneath the bed next to his. He reached out and grabbed one. The cover said *Sub-Mariner, Deep-Sea Avenger!* and featured a garish illustration of two creatures, half-fish and half-man, doing battle under the sea. As he sat up in the bed and began to read, Tomás asked, "Is it okay if he borrows that for a bit?"

"Those belong to Diaz, but he won't mind." Custodio sat down on a bed near the door. He leaned his crutch against the wall. "Can he read English?"

"He can't read it too well, but he speaks it just fine." Tomás nodded with his chin at Custodio's crutch. "What happened to your foot?"

"I twisted my ankle in an irrigation ditch." The boy's face turned red. "Felt like a fool. It happened the first day I was here. Claro, the mayordomo, was showing me how to position the ladder in the tree. I had my eye on him, and not the ground. I stepped right into the ditch that runs along the trees. Fell right on my face."

"You break anything?"

"No." Custodio looked down at the bandaged foot, as if to make sure it was still there. "It's just a sprain."

"There a doctor on the ranch?"

Custodio shook his head. "No, but Dallas took a look

at it. He told me it was nothing. Just need to lay off it for a while."

"For how long?"

"Not sure, exactly."

"They taking care of you in the meantime?"

"If I'm not picking, I'm not making any money." He nodded through the window to where you could see just the top of the rancher's house. "And they're charging me for meals, and for staying here."

"They're running a tab for you." Tomás laughed. "Hell, you're going to leave this place poorer than when you got here."

Now Custodio laughed. "That's not possible."

He glanced down again, but this time he was looking at the crate under his bed. Something inside the crate was moving. When he reached down with his right hand, Tomás heard whimpering.

"What have you got there?"

"My dog," Custodio said proudly as he pulled out a small white puppy. It had long floppy ears and kept touching its black nose with its tongue.

"My God, are you allowed to have pets in here?"

"Not exactly," said Custodio. "I took him from the barn. A dog showed up at the house last week and gave birth to a litter of puppies. This is one of them."

"And they let it sleep in the bunkhouse?"

Custodio's face reddened yet again.

"I only bring him in during the day, when the others are out picking." He raised up the puppy and called out to Juanito. "You can play with him if you want."

But Juanito didn't reply. He just threw the comic on the ground and reached for another.

"He doesn't like dogs," Tomás explained. "Or rabbits or mice or much of anything else. He's just not good at connecting with things. People or animals or whatever. Can't make eye contact. Can't feel what they're feeling. Maybe it's because of his size. Maybe he just don't want to, I don't know. But he won't want anything to do with your puppy."

Outside there was a noise. A car door opening, or maybe the hood from the Chevy down the road slamming down. Custodio rose to look out the window to see what it was, forgetting his bandaged foot. He winced with pain and quickly sat down.

Tomás leaned forward and said, "You sure you're okay?"

Custodio placed the puppy on the bed while he reached down to massage his ankle. "Yes, I think so. Anyway, Dallas said it was nothing."

"Well." Tomás turned from Custodio and looked around the room. "Unless this Dallas is a doctor, you don't know what's wrong. Why, I heard of guys twisting their ankle and thinking it was nothing. Some field boss told them to 'walk it off,' and that's just what they did.

Come to find out later it's a fracture. One guy I saw in El Centro couldn't even walk, on account of some bad medical advice he received. You're a young guy—you want to have a limp for the rest of your life?"

As Custodio shook his head, the puppy jumped and licked his fingers.

Tomás got off the bed and walked to the table at the back of the room. On top of the table, which was scratched and stained, laid a loose deck of cards. As he absentmindedly flipped through the cards, he asked, "Who is this Dallas, anyway?"

"He's Vaughn's boy. That's the rancher who owns this place."

Tomás turned over some cards. He grinned at an ace. He frowned at a two. "The boss's son, eh?"

Custodio nodded.

"What sort of man is he?"

"He's okay. Comes around a lot, even into the bunkhouse. He knows a little Spanish and tries to be friendly, always talking to the workers. He thinks it'll put the men at ease, but it does just the opposite."

Tomás nodded. He'd known the type. "They want you to think they're your best friend," he said. "Only they're a friend you have no choice but to have."

Juanito, oblivious to the conversation, chuckled at something in the comic and turned the page.

"Some of the men say he cheats us out of our wages,"

said Custodio. "That when the checks come, they're smaller than they should be."

"And that's because of this guy, Dallas?"

Custodio shrugged. "Who knows? But he's always poking his nose around. And he has a hand in everything. Payroll, picking the crews, you name it."

Tomás picked up the cards and shuffled them over and over. "Anybody ever stand up to this Dallas?"

"The men are afraid to. He's a powerful man, even if he's not big in size. No one wants to be seen as a trouble-maker, or get on Vaughn's bad side."

"Yeah, well, I hope I don't run into this Dallas."

"You will. He comes by all the time. His wife does, too."

Tomás stopped shuffling. "Wife?" He grinned. "Tell me about her."

"She's Mexican. Her name's Celedonia. From what I heard, she used to work here, over in the packing shed."

"You don't say. How long ago was that?"

"That she worked here? Oh, I don't know." The dog was now sleeping, his snores sounding like the purr of a cat. Custodio rubbed the puppy's belly with the back of his left hand. "One of the other men can tell you."

"She a looker?"

"Sometimes. Last Saturday night they went dancing in Santa Barbara. She got all dolled up and looked pretty fine. Other times I've seen her, she looked like any other girl who works in the packing shed."

"Yeah, except she doesn't work in the packing shed anymore." Tomás nodded again to the big house sitting at the end of the palm-lined driveway. "She lives in a mansion with the boss and the boss's son. That shows she's an attractive girl, no matter what she looks like."

Juanito, hearing the talk of Celedonia, put down the comic and pushed his way off the bed. He walked to where Tomás was standing.

"No, Tomás. No girls. You promised. We need to stay out of trouble so we can get to my uncle's."

"Relax, Juanito. I'm asking a few questions, that's all." He looked down at the cards again, still grinning. "I'm not saying I'm going to try my luck with her or anything."

Juanito stood there for a few seconds, just staring at his friend. Finally, he raised his left arm and slapped Tomás's hands. The cards went flying, showering the floor, landing on the table and chairs, ricocheting off the walls.

"Now, why'd you have to go and do that?"

As Tomás got down on his hands and knees and began to gather up the cards, Juanito began to pace back and forth. He mumbled and repeatedly bit one of his thumbnails. At one point, he stopped and slapped himself across the face, hard. The sound was like slapping a wet ham.

Custodio, still sitting on the bed with the sleeping puppy, watched them both with his mouth open.

As Juanito was about to slap himself again, the door to the bunkhouse flew open. Tomás, still on the ground picking up the cards, looked through the legs of the table and saw the legs of a man. Expensive brown cowboy boots and tan slacks, pressed.

A voice boomed out: "Where's Santos?"

Tomás stood up. Juanito, upon hearing the door open, had raced to a corner and turned to the wall as Custodio tried to hide the sleeping puppy with his pillow.

The man was old, tall and thin, with a long face that held a wispy white beard. Underneath his tan cowboy hat there was a tuft of white hair. His fair and freckled skin, deeply tanned, gave him an orange hue. He was hunched over, and his left hand moved with a constant tremor. When he spoke again, it was mostly underneath his breath, his words more like thoughts. He didn't expect the men in the room to understand English.

"Someone told me they'd seen someone come in here, so I thought maybe it was Santos."

Custodio rose with the help of his crutch and said, "Santos *no está aquí ahora mismo.*"

"No Santos?" Vaughn replied. "Just you three *muchachos*, eh?"

When no one else said anything, Juanito glanced to see if it was safe to turn around. Seeing the older man still standing in the middle of the room, he quickly turned back to the wall.

"Why, hello, big fella." The man approached Juanito slowly and carefully. He spoke loudly and slowly, as if that would help him be understood. "What's . . . your . . . name?"

Juanito turned, his eyes downcast and his chin firmly placed on his chest. "I'm—my name's Juanito."

"Well, what do you know. A wetback who speaks English, I'll be damned."

As the man stepped closer, Juanito began to shake. He raised a hand, as if to hit himself again, so Tomás stepped forward. "Good morning, sir. My name is Tomás Delgado and that's my friend, Juan Sanchez. We arrived this morning hoping to find work."

The man turned, approached Tomás and put out a hand weathered with age. When Tomás shook it, the man placed his other hand on Tomás's forearm. He squeezed and moved his hand up to Tomás's bicep. "Well, it's nice to meet you. My name's Vaughn. Wendell Vaughn. I own this ranch."

Tomás flashed a smile and took back his hand. The man then approached Juanito, patting him twice on the shoulder in two different places. Tomás knew the man was trying to seem friendly—the hand shaking and pats on the back—but he was just inspecting his new workers, like animals at an auction.

"He's a big fella, ain't he?" Vaughn pointed to Juanito. "Not sure I ever seen one so big, at least around here."

Tomás nodded and looked to the ground. Custodio, unable to follow the conversation, sat back down. He quickly scooped up the puppy and returned it to the crate under his bed.

"I'd ask if you two were related but, judging by his size and yours"—Vaughn laughed—"I'm guessing you ain't."

"No, sir, we're not related, but I've known him a long time. We're traveling together."

"Traveling together," Vaughn repeated, scratching his chin. "That's nice. We got too many guys come here alone. They pick the trees for a while, make a little scratch, and when they leave, they're still alone. That ain't no way to live."

"No, sir, it isn't."

"I don't know why that is. Guess I've never really thought about it, but I'm thinking about it now, and it's wrong."

A truck pulled up outside the bunkhouse. Vaughn turned. A tall man, a Mexican, entered the room. He was wearing an old cowboy hat stained with sweat and dirt, as well as work clothes and heavy boots covered in mud.

"Santos," Vaughn said, "just the man I was looking for."

"I came back to get some ladders. A few of them are broken and can't be used." Santos spoke English with a heavy accent. He shot glances at Tomás and Juanito, but turned again to Vaughn. "You were looking for me?"

Vaughn smiled wide, but then stopped. He realized that if Santos was in the bunkhouse, then he wasn't out in the orchards with the pickers. "Why did you come for the ladders yourself? I've told you I don't want you leaving the crews unsupervised."

"The men will be fine. Claro is there." Santos could see that this didn't satisfy him. "They're not children, Vaughn."

"You want to bet?"

"They're not even picking yet—there's still dew on the fruit. There's nothing for me to supervise except the men sitting around and smoking."

Vaughn shifted uneasily from foot to foot, his hand trembling. While he hated the idea of the workers being idle, he was at least glad they weren't getting paid for it.

"Anyway, Santos," he said, "I got a little job for you. You know the puppies that that bitch who showed up here last week saddled us with?"

Santos nodded.

"Well, I want you to get rid of them."

"All of them?"

"Yes. The mother, too, while you're at it. Goddamn freeloader."

Tomás, who'd been staring at the ground, raised his

face and turned to look at Vaughn. Vaughn didn't notice, his eyes on Santos.

"Kill them, you mean?" asked Santos, slowly. He wanted to make sure he understood the request.

Vaughn nodded, adding, "I don't want to seem hardhearted, but I can't have my ranch turned into a kennel. Already they're getting underfoot and creating problems. So I'd just rather you do away with the whole lot of them."

"Can't I just put them in the truck, drive them to the foothills, and ditch them?"

"I won't have you wasting my gas on account of some goddamn mutts."

Santos considered his options. "You have a gun I can use?"

"Don't be stupid, Santos. That'd make too much of a mess. Use the big tub behind the barn. The one we use to check for leaks in tires." He put a hand to his chin and figured. "Shouldn't take more than a couple of minutes per dog, I reckon. They're young and weak. Won't put up much of a fight."

"But, Vaughn, there are almost a dozen of them."

"Yeah, I know, and their constant yapping's keeping me up at night." The rancher's face turned red and his voice grew louder. "Look, I want them gone and if you can't handle the job, I'll find someone who can. And maybe I'll be looking to get me a new foreman while I'm at it."

Santos glanced around the room and hung his head. He finally said, "Yes, sir."

"Good, now that that's settled, why don't you get those ladders, as well as gear for these two new men, and get your ass back to the orchards where it belongs."

Santos slunk out of the room. Vaughn was just about to follow him when the puppy underneath Custodio's bed let out a yelp. Vaughn quickly turned, his left hand beginning to tremble wildly.

"Goddamnit, is that one of them?"

Custodio quickly put his hand down to silence the dog. Before Vaughn could say anything else, Dallas entered the room. He was a younger and smaller version of his father, the only differences being that his skin wasn't as tan and the hair that peeked out from under his cowboy hat was darker and more full.

"Dad, I heard you was in here."

"Am on my way out, Son. Was looking for Santos so he could take care of those goddamn mutts. He just left."

Dallas vaguely nodded. "Well, they're looking for you up at the house. The tax guy's here."

Dallas turned from his dad, finally noticing the strangers in the room.

"These fellas know English," Vaughn said with wonder, pointing to Tomás and Juanito.

Dallas pushed up his hat and stepped closer. "You don't say."

Vaughn nodded proudly, as if he was the owner of a pet who could do a special trick.

With another strange face in the room, Juanito became visibly uncomfortable. He pushed himself against the wall, hard, and began to writhe. Tomás stepped up and introduced himself and Juanito, same as he'd done for the father.

"Why, that's pretty amazing," Dallas said. "I never saw a picker who could speak English. Where you boys from?"

"Up north."

"Yeah, whereabouts? We got family up north, too."

"Hollister."

"I got an aunt in Salinas, but I've never been to Hollister. Nice town?"

"We liked it okay."

Dallas noticed the cards in Tomás's hands. "You play?"

Tomás nodded, reluctantly.

"I'm pretty good at poker." Dallas nodded at Custodio. "I tried playing with these boys, but they just ain't smart enough to keep up. But you, I got a good feeling about you. Maybe we could get a game going sometime."

"I'd like that," said Tomás.

Dallas began to speak again, but his father interrupted him.

"Son, are you through keeping the crew from their picking? Because Santos is about to take these boys out to the orchards."

The smile disappeared from Dallas's face. He backed away from Tomás. "Sorry, Dad," he said softly. "I'll run up to the house and tell the tax guy you'll be there shortly."

"You do that."

Dallas disappeared through the door. Vaughn shook his head, and was about to follow, when he looked to Custodio.

"Don't get too attached to that dog, you hear?" He then looked to Tomás. "You tell him what I said, okay? I want him to understand who runs things around here."

"I'll tell him," Tomás quietly replied.

"You better, or else I'll get two more guys in here so fast it'll make your head spin." He pointed to the beds with his thumb. "The hard part ain't getting a space in one of these bunks. The hard part is not losing your space to someone else, you get me?"

Tomás nodded.

Vaughn gave the room a final inspection and then opened the door to leave. Dallas was already halfway to the house, his footsteps kicking up clouds of dust as he ran.

A few seconds after Vaughn left, Tomás turned to his friend, scolding him in Spanish. "Juanito, I told you not to say anything."

"I'm sorry, Tomás." Juanito finally pushed himself from the wall. "I just couldn't—when he said hello, I just had to say something."

"'Just had to say something.' If you're not careful, you're going to mess this up for us the same way it got messed up in Goleta."

"That was you, Tomás." Juanito sat down on his bed. It creaked loudly. "That wasn't me, that was you."

"Well, whoever it was, if we ever plan on making it to Los Angeles with a bit of money, we need to keep our mouths shut and our noses clean—you hear me?"

Juanito jerked his head up and down fervently.

"He'll forget you," said Custodio as he reached his hand down to grab the dog. "There are too many men on the ranch. Not to mention the others that get picked up in the trucks every day." He kicked at the iron post of the bed next to his with his good foot. "We all look alike to him. He won't remember you."

"It's not him I'm worried about," said Tomás, "it's that son of his. If he's looking for a best friend, I'm not it."

"I don't like it here, Tomás," Juanito whined. "That man is mean. I want to go home."

Tomás turned to face his friend. "You don't have a home to go to, remember? Your aunt died. The bank took the house. We're going to see your uncle."

"Why can't we go now, Tomás?" Juanito looked

around the room, panicked. "This place is only going to lead to trouble, just like the last place."

"Shut up, Juanito," Tomás snapped. "I can't take your whining all the time."

"I should have gone on my own." Juanito spoke under his breath. "I could have been there by now. I should have gone on my own. I could have—"

There was a knock on the door. Custodio looked surprised, as if such formalities were a rarity on the ranch.

"Hello, is anybody in there?" It was a woman's voice. "I'm looking for my husband."

Custodio whispered, "That's Celedonia."

Juanito's and Custodio's faces clouded over, but Tomás just grinned. "Come on in," he said.

She opened the door and slowly entered. She looked around the room, as if she'd never visited the bunkhouse before.

She had a long nose and wavy hair that was dark red. Her skin was light brown and smooth. She looked about thirty. She was tall, almost as tall as her husband. A light cotton dress with a pattern of chevrons hung loosely on her slight frame. Tomás thought she looked like María Montez. He liked María Montez.

"Dallas went back to the house," Tomás said. "Vaughn, too. A few minutes ago."

"I must have just missed them. There's a path that leads from the back door to the dining hall and then to here." She looked out the window to the dirt road. "They must have gone the regular way."

"Well, they looked to me like regular guys."

Her face softened and she laughed. Tomás decided he liked her laugh.

"Who are you?" she asked.

"We showed up today looking for work. My name's Tomás, and that's Juanito."

She assessed them. "Pickers," she said plainly.

"How do you know I'm not the tax guy?"

She just laughed again and threw her head back. When she did, the waves of her hair bounced against her shoulders. Tomás almost sighed.

"You're funny," she said.

"I'm lots of things."

Celedonia was about to say something else when she stopped and just smiled instead.

"You got any tips for us? I heard that you used to work here, too."

Her smile quickly disappeared. "That was years ago."

"Yeah, but the thing about the fields is, they never change. Believe me, I've seen enough of them to know."

Celedonia walked around the room. She peered underneath the beds, inspecting the meager belongings of the men. "Why didn't you ever try for more?"

"How do you know I didn't?"

"You wouldn't be here if you had."

She circled the table, pausing at the poster of the Virgin of Guadalupe. She approached Juanito, who cringed at her presence.

"He don't talk much," Tomás called out. "Especially to women."

Celedonia kept moving toward him. Juanito shut his eyes tight.

"My god, he's big." She turned to Tomás. "Does he wrestle? Imagine him in the ring. He could easily break a man's neck."

"He doesn't like sports much. Plus, he's not violent. Might have had an easier time if he had been. He could have stuck up for himself more as a kid."

Turning back to Juanito, Celedonia said, "The men here watch the fights on Wednesday nights. On channel 5 in the dining hall. It makes me sick."

"Yeah, well," said Tomás, "I don't know about all of that kind of thing. I'm a lover, not a fighter."

Celedonia gave a small smile and walked down the aisle between the beds. For a second it looked like she was going to sit down, but then she thought better of it. "I have to be going."

"So soon?" Tomás stepped toward her. He hoped to smell some of her perfume, but all he got was the bunkhouse.

She blushed. "They'll be waiting for me at the house."

"Let them wait."

As she walked toward the door, Tomás was beside her. "Maybe I'll see you around sometime."

Celedonia smiled. "Maybe you will."

Tomás followed her out the door. He leaned against the side of the bunkhouse and watched her walk away. He figured that maybe he'd gotten to her a little bit, and that as she was walking she was thinking about him. He wanted to see if she'd look back. If she looked back, then he'd know.

Celedonia was just about at the end of the dirt road he and Juanito had walked down earlier that day. The sun was high in the sky, and it was much warmer than it was that morning. The mountains loomed in the background, brown and red and green. As she turned, and headed toward the driveway that led to the house, she looked back. Tomás had his answer.

He was still grinning when Santos pulled up a few minutes later. He was driving a black Ford flatbed truck with a small trailer. The trailer held four orchard ladders along with picking sacks, sleeves, and gloves.

"I got all your gear," Santos called out through the open window, "along with a couple of lunches. You guys can ride up in the cab with me." Nodding to the bunkhouse, he added, "If you think your friend will fit. Otherwise, he can just climb in the back."

A canopy had been constructed on the back of the

truck, the beige canvas stained with dirt. Two benches ran the length of the space.

"Come on, Juanito." Tomás kicked the bunkhouse door with his foot. "Time to go to work."

Juanito slowly came out of the bunkhouse, followed by Custodio with the crutch under his arm. The puppy was on his shoulder, nuzzling and licking his ear.

As Juanito and Tomás climbed into the truck, Santos called out, "You'd better not get too attached to that dog, Custodio."

"What, to Palomo?" Custodio reached up and tickled the puppy's chin. The dog responded by yelping and licking his long fingers. "He's not going anywhere."

Santos just shook his head and put the truck into gear. After it rumbled down the dirt road and turned onto the blacktop, heading for the orchards, all was quiet again. The car that was being repaired was gone. There was no sign of Vaughn or Dallas or Celedonia. The men wouldn't be back for hours, and Custodio had a bit of free time before he needed to start what few chores he was able to perform.

He went back inside the bunkhouse. He noticed that Diaz's comic books were sitting on the floor where Juanito had dropped them. He'd clean those up later. He let the crutch fall to the ground and sat on the bed, playing with the dog. It licked his face and erupted in little yelps whenever Custodio scratched its belly.

"Don't you mind what that mean old man said," Custodio told the little dog. "I'll protect you."

S ANTOS DROVE THEM to an orchard a few miles
away. The road was narrow, just two lanes. The only
other vehicle they passed was a truck from one of the
other ranches. Santos waved at the driver. The driver nodded and waved back.

The truck slowed and pulled off the road. Lemon trees
stretched for hundreds of yards to the left and right. If
you looked directly down one of the rows, all you saw
were trees until the land blurred into mountains. Above
was a blue sky streaked with clouds.

The trees were about twelve feet tall, with long leaves
that were curled and had light-green veins running down
the middle. The trunks were hidden in the foliage, so the
trees looked more like giant bushes. They'd been planted
about ten feet apart, which was just wide enough for a
truck to drive down. The lane between the trees was lit-
tered with pruned branches and lemons that had ripened
too soon. A shallow irrigation ditch ran along the line of
trees.

Santos climbed down from the truck, and Tomás and

Juanito got out on the other side. Juanito looked around, blinking. Tomás sighed. It was quiet except for the chatter and banter of the men who were picking trees a couple of rows over.

Claro saw them and came over. He was dark-skinned and wearing work clothes. Underneath his cowboy hat he wore a faded red bandanna wrapped around his head.

"I gave the men the go-ahead to get started. The fruit seemed dry enough." He looked up to the sky, and then back to Santos. "I didn't want to lose the whole day."

Santos nodded in agreement and walked to the trailer hitched to the back of the truck. Tomás and Juanito followed. Santos pointed to two ladders that were sitting on top of a pile of gear.

"Here's everything you'll need." He turned to Juanito. "I sure hope we have something that fits him."

Tomás said, "Don't worry, we'll make it work."

Santos followed Claro to the trees that had just been picked. Santos looked them over. The trees still had fruit on them. Any lemon that either was the wrong size, or wasn't ready to be picked, stayed on the tree. Santos was making sure none of the men had skipped the harder-to-reach fruit at the top of the tree.

Satisfied, he walked back to Tomás and Juanito. Santos dug two nibs of chalk out of his pocket. He gave one to Tomás and the other to Juanito. He assigned them the numbers on the ladders. This is what they'd write on every box they filled to get paid for what they picked.

Santos then assigned them each a section of eight trees. Tomás nodded and made sure Juanito knew which trees were his. Juanito nodded his head vaguely, never looking up.

Tomás reached into the trailer for a pair of thick gloves that had large cuffs intended to protect the wrist. He helped Juanito stretch them over his huge hands. He also showed Juanito how to pull on the heavy canvas sleeve for protecting his arm from the sharp thorns of the branches as he reached in for the fruit. On most men, the sleeve covered all the way up to the shoulder. On Juanito, it barely went up to his elbow.

Tomás went back to the trailer and grabbed one of the picking sacks. He put it on, draping it down the front of his body and putting the thick strap over his left shoulder. The heavy canvas bag was the size of an apron, and at the top, there was a reinforced leather lip that gave the pouch some shape so that lemons could be dropped in without having to search for the opening at the top. Halfway down the sack were two buckles, one on either side, sealing the bottom of the bag so that the lemons could be deposited into the crates without the picker taking off the bag.

He grabbed a pair of clippers and a sizing ring, showing Juanito how to hold each. Walking up to a tree, Tomás showed how the picking was done in one fluid motion. First you sized the lemon with the ring, clipped it just above the stem, and then dropped it into your sack.

As Tomás was doing this a car went by, a convertible. Juanito turned to watch it pass. The radio was blasting "Toolie Oolie Doolie," and the tune seemed to hang in the air for a few seconds after the car was gone.

"For God's sake, pay attention," Tomás snapped. "If you don't pick anything, you won't get paid anything. You hear me?"

Juanito turned back to his friend, who repeated the demonstration. Tomás then showed him how to plant the pole of the ladder inside the tree and how to climb, steadying himself with one hand while clipping and picking the fruit with the other. Juanito just kicked at the mulch collected between the rows of trees.

Tomás climbed down and grabbed Juanito's sack and ladder out of the trailer. He adjusted the strap on the sack so that it was as big as it could be. Tomás handed it to Juanito since he couldn't reach above his friend's head to put it on. On Juanito, it looked like a baby's bib. He handed him the orchard ladder and told him, "Start low, pick the inside, then use the ladder for the top stuff. You understand?"

Juanito nodded, but it was the same nod he always gave. You could tell him that the sun orbited the earth, or that the moon was made of cheese, and Juanito would give that same nod. Tomás had seen it hundreds of times. He just shrugged and pointed Juanito to his section.

For most men, carrying the ladder was awkward and difficult. It weighed only about forty pounds, but it was tall and unwieldy. Juanito carried it as if it were weightless.

Picking his first tree, he was too rough, plunging in with his whole body and snapping off branches as he lunged for the fruit. He also wasn't paying attention to which lemons he picked. Tomás told him to slow down, showing him again how to use the sizing ring and to only pick the lemons that matched it.

Once he got the hang of it, Juanito was fast and efficient. Being so tall, and with such long arms, he saved time by not having to go up and down the ladder. He could just stand on the first rung and reach any branch. In no time, he'd picked ten boxes and caught up to the other men.

Tomás struggled to keep up, and once or twice, Claro came over and yelled at him for leaving behind good fruit. Swearing under his breath, Tomás barely managed to keep up with the group.

Most of the pickers were in their late twenties or early thirties. They looked more like Tomás than Juanito, with dark skin, jet-black hair and deep-set facial features. They all wore hats along with boots and heavy jeans.

The men were constantly on the move. Positioning

their ladders, emptying their lemons, moving on to the next tree. Occasionally a picker would disappear to urinate, keeping his sack on while he peed, but he was soon up his ladder again and back to work. One of the men followed the pickers and stacked up the filled crates four high. A truck would come by later and take all the boxes to the packing shed.

As the men picked, methodically working their way through their sections, Santos built a fire in the middle of the box row. Once the fire had a chance to burn, he called the men in for lunch.

The pickers left the ladders where they were and emptied whatever lemons they had in their sacks into a box. Taking off their picking sacks, every worker had dark lines of sweat across their front and in a line on their back from where the bag and strap had been. They each unwrapped their lunch, tortillas filled with pork, beans, and rice, and placed them on the hot coals of Santos's fire.

As they sat and ate their food, the workers all marveled at the size of Juanito. They asked him questions and joked about how big he was. He was uncomfortable being the center of attention, so Tomás answered anything that was asked. Soon, he was forgotten as a novelty and the men kidded each other and boasted, giving the slower workers a hard time for not filling more boxes or pretending to have picked more than they did. When they finished their lunch, each man took a drink from a huge drum bolted onto a corner of the flatbed, filling up a tin cup attached with a length of twine to the truck's bumper.

The rest of the day followed the same as before, the men working quickly, picking lemons, filling crates, and carrying their ladders to the next tree. The day became hotter and Juanito began to turn red under the harsh sun. Claro took pity on him and gave him his hat. One or two men took breaks to smoke or take gulps of water from the truck, but they always shuffled quickly back to their trees, their lemon sacks hanging off them like giant appendages.

At a little before five, Santos put his fingers in his mouth and whistled. The men emptied the last of their lemons into crates, wrote their numbers in chalk for the last time that day, and headed back to the truck with their ladders. After depositing the ladders in the trailer behind the truck, the men—one by one and clutching their lemon sacks, gloves, and sleeves—climbed onto the flatbed. Even though they were exhausted and covered with dust and sweat, they still kidded and gave each other a hard time.

"Diaz, you barely picked twenty boxes today. My sick old grandmother could pick more than that."

"Pedro, you damned coyote. I saw you trying to write your number on my crates."

"Guillermo, you went behind a tree and didn't come out for twenty minutes. Did you take a shit or a nap?"

Because it was Friday, there was relief in knowing that

they'd only pick a half day on Saturday and that Sunday meant no picking at all.

On the road back to the ranch, they passed a number of other trucks headed to Santa Paula, Oxnard, and Ventura, the day's picking done. Hundreds of men would soon return to street corners or the labor camps.

Santos dropped off the men at the dining hall and drove to where he parked the truck overnight near the packing shed.

The dining hall was a long wooden building behind the bunkhouses. Dinner consisted of pretty much the same thing they had for lunch, only served with coffee instead of water. The men ate quickly, wiped the plates clean with a tortilla, and then lounged around outside, smoking and talking. In the field behind the packing shed, a few men tossed around a baseball. Others watched and encouraged the players while picking their teeth with splinters from the wooden boxes that held the lemons.

Santos, having parked the truck and filed his paperwork, was on his way to dinner. He called out to a few of the men as he walked, thanking them for their work that day. His voice caught the ear of Vaughn, who was on his back porch listening for him.

"Santos, is that you?"

Santos stopped and looked up at the sky. He contemplated not answering, but knew Vaughn would just track him down at the bunkhouse later, the way he'd already done earlier in the day.

"Yes, Vaughn," Santos called out in English. "What can I do for you?"

Santos stood there for the minute or two it took the old man to walk down the path from the rear of his house. As he waited, men passed by on their way to the dining hall. All of them nodded to Santos as they passed.

When Vaughn finally emerged from the shaded path, he was walking with the aid of a cane. He was wearing the same clothes as earlier in the day, except he was missing his hat. Santos could see through his thinning hair to the freckled and dried scalp below.

"The dogs," Vaughn said, "I thought I told you to get rid of those goddamn dogs."

Workers leaving and entering the dining hall went out of their way to walk around Vaughn and Santos.

"I was in the orchards all day." Santos pointed back toward the packing shed. "I just brought back the truck."

"Well then, what are you waiting for?"

Santos didn't want to say it. He knew the rancher wasn't going to care. "I'm on my way to—can I just eat first?"

"You can have your supper when you're done with your goddamn job, or else you won't have a job." Vaughn lifted the cane and brought it back to the ground. A small cloud of dust rose from the indentation created. "Keep in mind, Santos, I'm the one who provides your meals. And the roof over your head. So unless you want to lose both right this second, you'll do what I say."

Santos seemed to shrink under the verbal assault. He replied with a meager, "Yes, sir," turned away from the dining hall, and walked off in the direction of the barn.

Vaughn called after him, leaning heavily on the cane. His raised hand trembled. "I want all of them gone, Santos. Every last mutt on this ranch, gone!"

After Santos disappeared behind a row of trees, the rancher suddenly felt self-conscious. Hearing men leaving the dining hall, he began to hobble back to the house, cursing under his breath.

Tomás watched Vaughn as he retreated. Juanito was standing next to him, staring down at the ground. Claro approached from the dining hall.

"Hey, your friend's quite a worker." He pointed toward Juanito, who began to walk ahead of them, his chin pressed into his chest like always. Juanito's shirt had dark sweat stains, and his boots and jeans were covered in dirt. All the men were similarly filthy. Only their faces, which they'd wiped down in the communal bathroom before they ate, were clean. "I never seen a guy that large move so fast."

"Yeah, Juanito may not be too smart, but he'll do what you tell him." Tomás turned, and they began to walk toward the bunkhouse. "And for a big guy, he can be light on his feet."

The day had cooled off, the bright sun from before now low on the horizon and half-hidden by clouds. The sunset gave the entire ranch a pink hue. Behind them, more men were exiting the dining hall. They were laughing, joking, smoking.

"You guys been traveling around together long?"

"I've known him since he was a kid, up in Hollister. But this is the first time I've ever gone anywhere with him. Hell"—he kicked at the ground as he walked—"for all I know, it's the first time he's been anywhere."

Claro shot him a quizzical look.

"He grew up with his aunt. She never really let him out of the house. Juanito's kind, and can figure things out, but he doesn't know the way the world works."

They turned the corner, heading to the dirt road that led to the line of adobe bunkhouses.

"I guess she was trying to protect him," Tomás continued. "Protected him too much, I'd say. She died last month. But he's got an uncle down in Los Angeles. He agreed to look after Juanito and give him a job in a store that he has. That's where we're heading."

They approached the bunkhouse. Juanito went inside, the creaking of the old bed as he laid down audible even outside. Instead of entering, Claro and Tomás turned and just leaned against the front of the bunkhouse. The dirt road seemed to have even more tire tracks than that morning. The ranch never stopped.

"Where you guys been before now?"

"Up in Goleta," Tomás answered, grinning. "Picking lettuce, only we had to make a hasty getaway on account of a young girl there whose father didn't approve of me."

Now Claro grinned. "They never do, do they?"

"No, they sure don't." Tomás turned serious. "It's just his disapproval came at the wrong time. We'd been working there almost two weeks, and were just about to get our pay. But then we got run off."

"That's some bad luck."

"Only kind of luck I seem to have." Tomás nodded toward the inside of the bunkhouse. "Juanito was livid. Kept going on about how I'd broken my promise and let him down. I swear, he's like a goddamn kid sometimes. He looks at you with those brown eyes and starts crying."

"Crying? A big guy like him?"

"Well, not tears, you know. But the look that kids can give, with the bottom lip all puffed out. Juanito's still got that, let me tell you. And when he gives it to you, it makes you feel smaller than small."

"I know what you mean. I have little ones myself." Claro reached into his back pocket and pulled out a wallet. It was thin and made of old brown leather. When he opened it, there was nothing inside but photos. He flipped to one of a boy and two girls dressed in ill-fitting clothes and smiling widely for the camera. The youngest one was missing his front teeth. "It breaks my heart to leave them, but what can I do?"

Tomás glanced over at the picture, but then turned back to the dirt road. He tried to follow the deep ruts from where they started near the two-lane road to where they disappeared around the corner.

"You see them much?"

Claro spit at the ground. "I travel home when I can. The youngest one I've only seen once. The mother, she gives me hell when I go, but it's not more than I give myself."

He put away the wallet quickly, as if the longer he held it, the more pain it caused.

"Anyway, what can be done about it? It's just the way things are."

"Yeah," Tomás said under his breath, "but it's not the way things have to be."

Claro was about to speak when there was a loud noise. A yelp and a shout and a door slamming. They turned and saw Santos emerge from the barn with a large dog in his arms.

"Jesus," Tomás said, "that bastard rancher's really going to make him kill all them damn dogs."

The large dog was whimpering and yelping, despite Santos placing his hand over its mouth. Santos carried the dog around to the back of the barn. Seconds later, there was splashing, wailing, dying.

Claro ran his hand against the back of his neck and said, "I don't want to hear this."

Now Tomás spat at the ground. "Hearing death's better than seeing it. I was in the war. There was plenty of it."

Claro turned his eyes from the barn to Tomás. "You kill anyone?"

"Nah, my ship just accompanied the big destroyers. But you saw it from a distance. Heard it. Kind of like now. You knew it was happening not too far away from where you were."

"And that made it okay?"

Tomás looked at him. "Nothing made it okay, except that it wasn't you. Come on, let's go inside."

Claro followed Tomás into the bunkhouse.

Juanito was on his bed, reading another issue of *Sub-Mariner*. The cover showed a woman in a red dress tied to a buoy. A torpedo, labeled ATOMIC, was flying out of the water and headed her way. Custodio, his crutch leaning against the wall, was playing with his puppy.

Sitting down on his bed, Claro asked, "What did you mean, what you said before?"

Tomás walked to the back of the room and sat down on one of the chairs. "What'd I say?"

"That it wasn't how it had to be."

"I just meant, for Juanito and me. We're going to stop

running. Stop killing ourselves in these fields and picking food for people who spit on us. Hell, you know what some guy called me in the navy? A ground-nigger." He kicked at the floor. "As if that makes any kind of sense."

"But what will you do? Where will you go?"

Tomás nodded toward Juanito. "Like I said, he has an uncle in Los Angeles. There's a whole community of Mexicans down there. And they have real jobs. Movie theaters. Hotels. Markets. Juanito's uncle has a little grocery store, and that's where we're going to work. Live, too. He has a few rooms above, right on Soto Street. It should be real nice, and we won't have some grower on our backs all the time. Hell, those ranchers care more about their damn trees than they do about us."

Claro chuckled. "I don't even think they care about the trees, except that they make them money."

The door opened and slammed against the wall. Santos stood in the opening, his shirt and the top of his pants wet.

"Custodio," he said darkly, "give me the dog."

"My puppy?" Custodio held it to his chest. The dog could sense that something was wrong. He began to whimper. "You can't take Palomo. He's mine."

As Santos approached, the sound of his boots on the wooden floor seemed to echo. There was no other sound. Even Juanito had put down his comic book and was paying attention.

"Goddamnit, son," Santos barked, "give me that dog. Vaughn's given me orders, and I have to follow them."

"Oh, come on, Santos," Claro interjected. "You just tell old Wendell he can go straight to—"

Santos turned quickly and raised his hand. "Don't get involved, Claro, or else you'll lose your job, too. Vaughn would replace both of us in a second, you know that."

Claro closed his mouth and stared at the floor.

Santos began to advance again toward Custodio. The puppy, already nuzzling the boy's chest, began to crawl inside his denim shirt for safety. Custodio tried to stand, except his crutch was leaning against the wall. He sat down in pain.

Santos stood above him and reached for the dog. After a brief struggle, he pulled it out of the younger man's hands. The dog cried out in a high-pitched yelp that gave everyone in the room chills. Santos, the dog writhing in his arms, looked around the bunkhouse and then stormed out. Custodio fell against his mattress, turned toward the wall, and began to sob.

Tomás said quietly, "I never saw such a thing."

Claro, as if snapping out of a trance, said, "Let me go and speak to him. Santos wouldn't do such a thing, no matter what Vaughn told him."

He left the bunkhouse, muttering about the rancher under his breath.

"Tomás," Juanito whimpered, "I don't like it here. We need to get to my uncle's."

Tomás turned to his friend. "I know, Juanito. And we will. We just need to make some money first. And then we'll say goodbye to these goddamn fields and orchards forever."

"You promise, Tomás? You really promise?"

"Hell yeah, Juanito." He reached down and slapped at the cuffs of his pants. A cloud of dust rose from his jeans. "You think I want to break my back picking fruit for the rest of my life? Or lettuce or almonds or anything? Not me. Not us. Let the rest of these guys ruin their bodies and fill their lungs with pesticides, but you and me, Juanito, we're cut out for better things."

"Stop running," Juanito said. He was smiling wildly and rocking back and forth. "We're going to belong."

"You bet, old buddy. We're going to be permanent. Have a real roof over our heads, and a nice room to sleep in. One that won't be filled with dirt and spiders. Or that smells like sweat. We're going to live like real human beings, and not dogs. Not anymore." Tomás's voice was low and steady, as if he were talking in his sleep. "You and me, we're finally going to get to live like everyone else. In a real town with real jobs. Be real men. Live real lives."

Juanito was nodding and smiling when Claro came back into the bunkhouse. He looked stunned. "Damned if he didn't do it."

Tomás knew what he was referring to, and didn't want to know any more.

But Juanito asked, "Do what?"

"Killed all them dogs. Even the pups. Even Custodio's. Goddamn spineless bastard."

"Santos is your friend," Tomás said, "don't speak of him that way. You'd have done the same thing if the rancher had ordered you to, and you know it."

"You should see them all, out behind the barn. There's more than a dozen of them. Wet and lifeless. They look like puppets, or toys. Stupid, senseless death." He turned and looked at Tomás. "Vaughn wouldn't even let Santos bury them. Ordered him to just throw them in with the garbage and food scraps."

"Tomás," Juanito whined.

"I know," he said, "I know. You don't like it here. Well, I don't like it here much either. But we got to stick around for a little while longer. Get a little money in our pockets. Then we can go."

Claro sniffed and wiped away something from his eyes. He turned again to Tomás. "Listen, tomorrow night a bunch of us are going into Ventura. There are a few good bars downtown, and there's a pool hall we sometimes visit. And there's a movie theater. What do you say we get out of here for a couple of hours?"

Tomás picked up the deck of cards from the table.

He absentmindedly flipped through them. "Thanks, but I can't. Me and Juanito are broke."

"Movies," Juanito said, "I want to go to the movies."

Tomás turned to face him. "We're broke, Juanito. What have I just been saying?"

"You just think about it. But I know I need to get away from this awful place for a bit." Claro turned toward the door. "I'm going to try and find Santos. You're right about what you said. If Vaughn asked me to jump in the river, I'd pretty much have to do it. Not only that, I'd stay under the water until he told me I could come up for air."

He left the bunkhouse. Tomás started shuffling the cards while Juanito returned to his comic book.

"Did you mean all of that?"

Tomás had to look around to see where the words had come from. Custodio was still facing the wall. His voice sounded weak and small.

"Mean all of what?"

He turned over and faced Tomás.

"What you told Claro before. And your friend just now. About Los Angeles. Your friend's uncle. Leaving the fields. Did you mean all that?"

"Now, look," Tomás sounded annoyed, "I don't like anyone listening in on my private conversations."

Custodio rolled his eyes and pointed to the room. "Look around you. You can't have any secrets in a place like this."

Tomás grinned and leaned back. "Sure, I meant it. Wouldn't have said it if I didn't."

Custodio sat up and swung his legs over the side of the bed. He dropped his bandaged foot carefully to the floor. "I'd like to go to a place like that. I want to have a real job, too. Can I go with you?"

Tomás's grin disappeared. "What I was talking about, what you heard, that's just for Juanito and me."

"But can't I go along, too?"

"You got a job here, don't you?"

"Not for long. At least, not while I'm like this." Custodio raised his leg. "Since I can't pick, the rancher's going to cancel my contract. Will happen any day now. They could send me back to Mexico, or else to some place a lot worse than this."

"Send you back, how? If they called Immigration, they'd lose half these other guys, too. Then who'd pick their lemons?"

Custodio shook his head. "I'm a bracero, which means they can do whatever they want with me."

"But you got a contract, you said so yourself. That's got to protect you somehow."

He laughed darkly. "A lot of things were promised in that contract. A living wage. A clean place to live."

Tomás looked around the bunkhouse. "This place is not so bad. I've seen worse."

"I have, too. Believe me. And that's nowhere I want to go back to."

From across the room, Juanito lowered the comic and asked, "What's a *bracero*?"

Custodio seemed ashamed to say, so Tomás answered for him. "It's something they started during the war. The growers all panicked when the draft started and men got shipped away. They were worried there'd be no one left to pick their crops, not that G. I. Joe ever spent much time in the fields. So they set up a program with the government to get workers from Mexico. Basically, they shipped to America all the help they needed. Of course, they put in for twice as many workers than was required to do the job. That meant that wages went down for everyone. What a goddamn racket."

"But the war's been over for years." Juanito pointed to Custodio. "What's he still doing here?"

"The growers got used to it. They liked having workers they could easily pick on and exploit. You and me, we may be Mexicans, but at least we're citizens. We got options, even if we're broke. We can come and go as we please, and choose where we work. These poor devils, the braceros—they're bought and sold just like the slaves used to be. Treat them like trash. Treat them like cattle. Who cares? Mexico doesn't want them, and the ranchers don't really want them either, except during the harvest."

Tomás softened his tone and turned back to Custodio. "How'd you get wound up in such a thing?"

He shrugged. "We heard there was work in America. Everyone in the small villages did. It paid better than we had in Mexico, so I went."

"Where are you from?"

"I'm originally from Zacatecas, but we shipped out of the processing center in Empalme. It took almost all my money just to get there. I was naive in thinking I would get right on a list and be shipped out. Some men had been waiting there for three months. They were begging for food and eating banana peels out of the garbage. It was an awful sight. For the first few days I had to pay a peso for a place to sleep. I didn't know how long I'd be there, so for nearly a week I didn't eat."

Juanito heard this. He put the comic down and asked, "You didn't eat for a week?"

Custodio gravely nodded.

Juanito frowned, and went back to reading the comic.

"I finally couldn't wait anymore," Custodio continued, "so I gave my last ten dollars to one of the men who worked there and they put my name on the list. Once I got inside, I knew it'd been a mistake."

Tomás leaned forward. "What happened?"

"The processing of the men was brutal. They took our fingerprints, as if we were criminals. Then they tested us for venereal disease and tuberculosis. They examined our lungs and kidneys and our hearts but, most of all, our limbs. They wanted to make sure we could work. If you weren't strong or you had a bad back, they didn't want you. We were nothing more than animals to them. But the last stage was the worst. Every man had to undress, and while we stood there naked, they sprayed us with DDT."

"Goddamn, they fumigated you. Like you were a herd of goats."

"At the end, they made us sign a contract. Most of the men I was with couldn't read and only signed their name with a fingerprint. They didn't know what they were signing. They didn't care, they just wanted to work."

"How did you finally get to the States?"

"At Empalme they herded us onto boxcars to take us to the reception centers in America." Custodio's voice became slow and dreamy, as if what he was telling were just a story and not actually what had happened to him. "The journey lasted for hours, but all they gave us was one piece of white bread and a cup of coffee that tasted like it came out of the sewer."

"What happened when you got here?"

"I was traveling with two of my brothers, and a few other men from our village. We begged them to let us stay together, but no one would listen. No one cared. We were separated, every single one of us. One of my brothers was sent to Vallejo. Another was shipped to somewhere down near Orange County. Anaheim, I think. When I tried to ask why they were doing it, they just told me to shut up and be thankful I had a job."

Outside, men returning from dinner entered the other bunkhouses. Doors slammed, beds creaked.

"I was first sent to the Imperial Valley to pick sugar beets. It was summer and very hot. There was a bucket of water at each end of the field, but you couldn't have a drink until you were done. And if anyone stood up, to stretch or get a moment's relief, the foreman would yell at you to bend back down. At night my back would be on fire from working with that small hoe all day."

He shivered, as if he were still there. "I saw workers spitting foam from their mouths. I saw old men and women, even children, pass out because of the heat. It beat anything I'd ever seen in Mexico. The worst days of my life were spent in those fields."

"Did they at least give you a nice place to sleep?"

"It was a shack, with not even space enough to stretch. Men slept on the floor because they ran out of beds. I woke up more tired than before." Custodio bent over and held his head in his hands. "I don't know which was worse, being out in the field or being cooped up like an animal in the bunkhouse."

Tomás looked for something positive to say. "But—the money."

"There was no money. Even if you picked a hundred

boxes, once they took out what you owed for the blanket and your room and food, there was nothing left. Some men ended up owing more than they earned. How can you send anything home when you're not getting anything yourself?" He slammed his hand down on the bed, but it made no sound. "I got a check once for seven cents. Can you believe that? For a week's work. All of that blood and sweat, for nothing. For worse than nothing."

Juanito finished the comic, reached over, grabbed another.

"I can't do that for the rest of my life. No one should have to do that." Custodio raised his head and said, his voice filled with pleading, "That's why I want to go with you two."

Tomás looked surprised. "But you can't just leave. You have a contract, you said so yourself."

Custodio shrugged. "Sure, but I'd skip if I thought I could do better. A lot of the men do it."

"I don't know." Tomás kneaded his chin with his hand and felt his whiskers. They'd left Goleta in such a rush the day before that he didn't even have a toothbrush or a razor. All that he owned in the world he was wearing on his back. "What if Juanito's uncle doesn't have space for all three of us? Or enough work?"

"Nothing can be worse than what I've already lived through." He looked around the room. "Anywhere is better than here."

Tomás considered it. "You really want to go with us to Los Angeles?"

Custodio eagerly nodded.

"Yeah, but"—Tomás pointed to Custodio's leg—"what about your foot? Neither me nor Juanito's uncle is running a charity ward."

"I should be able to walk on it in a day or so." Custodio stood up, putting weight on both of his feet. He winced a bit but remained standing. "See? I can't do much, not at first, but I'd be able to help a little."

"Well, we'll see. On payday I guess I can—"

"Forget payday." Custodio reached into his meager basket of things and pulled out a wad of bills. "I have this, from when I hurt my leg. Santos wanted to take me into town to see a doctor, but Vaughn said that'd cost too much money. So Dallas gave me this to keep me quiet."

"What are you saying?"

"I'm saying we can leave now. Tonight." He turned the money over and over in his hands. Tomás followed it with his eyes. "This is more than enough for bus fare. I'll give the rest to Juanito's uncle, just to show I'm good for it."

Tomás smiled. He grabbed the money from Custodio's hand. "Hell, boy, I think we may just have ourselves a plan. Juanito," Tomás called out, "you want to leave tonight?"

"Right now?" Juanito said, sitting up on his bed. He smiled wide. "Leave?"

"Yes," Tomás answered.

A voice suddenly said, in English, "Go? Go where?"

All three of them looked toward the door of the bunkhouse. It was open, Dallas standing half-inside, half-outside. He was dressed differently from earlier in the day. Now he was wearing dark-blue jeans and a red western-styled shirt that had white piping decorating the front and back in curly lines. He looked like an extra in a bad movie about cowboys and Indians.

"Sorry, I thought that's what I heard." He stepped inside the room. "*Vámonos*, right?"

Tomás quickly pocketed the money. Juanito lay back down and resumed reading the comic book, while Custodio grabbed his crutch and hobbled out of the room as fast as he could.

"I didn't mean to get in the way of anything," Dallas said.

"No, it's okay. Custodio there was just heading out for a walk. That's what we were talking about."

"I didn't mean to eavesdrop, it's just"—Dallas looked sheepish—"I speak a little Spanish."

"I bet the men really appreciate it."

"You'd think so, but they don't." He looked to the door and then back toward Tomás. "I heard about that boy's pup. I'm real sorry about that, but when my dad gets something in his head, it's real hard to get it out."

Tomás waved his hand. "It's an attachment he

shouldn't have formed. After all, he was warned, was he not? He's just a boy. He'll get over it."

"I'm happy to hear you say that." Dallas motioned toward where the cards sat on the table. "You still up for a game?"

"Game?" asked Tomás.

"Yeah, remember? You said you played a little poker. Well, I do, too."

Dallas walked the length of the bunkhouse and sat down on one of the chairs. Tomás sighed and collected the cards. He quickly shuffled and dealt ten cards, five to Dallas and five to himself. Picking up his hand, Dallas looked around the room in awe. It was the first time he'd ever sat down in one of the bunkhouses. "Your name's Tomás, right?"

"Yes, Mr. Vaughn."

Dallas frowned. He threw down a pair of cards, took two new ones. "Call my dad Mr. Vaughn. My name's Dallas, and I want you to use it."

Tomás got rid of only one card. He drew its replacement slowly, looking at Dallas. "Okay, I will. Tell me, why are you called that?"

"Dallas, you mean?"

Tomás nodded and then called. Dallas showed his hand. Tomás beat him with three of a kind. Dallas frowned and waited for Tomás to deal a new hand.

"My dad was born and raised in Texas. Just outside of

Dallas, actually. He came here when he was a boy, but he still talks about it. I even got a brother named Austin, though he died. So he named us, I guess, to remind him of where he came from. You ever been to Texas?"

Tomás shook his head. "Arizona was the first place my family worked when they came over, but they moved to California pretty shortly after that."

"So then, you were born here?"

"Yes, in California." Tomás looked up from his cards. "Just like you."

Dallas made a face. Trying to change the subject, he asked, "So, how do you like our ranch?"

Tomás looked around the bunkhouse as Dallas examined his cards. "It's not bad."

"I know the men are always bellyaching about the work or the hours, but we do right by our workers, let me tell you." He got rid of a few cards and took new ones. "You should see the labor camps up north. They're worse than before the war, when there were those damn Okies and hoboes everywhere."

Tomás showed his hand. Dallas threw down his cards with confidence. He won with a straight flush. Tomás didn't react. He just swept up the cards and dealt again.

"Yeah, I'm glad it's all Mexicans now." Dallas inspected his new hand. "They make the best workers. You should be proud."

"To be Mexican?" Tomás asked, wryly. "Or to be considered a good worker?"

"Now, don't get fresh with me, boy. I'm giving you a compliment. We've been doing this a long time. My dad remembers when Filipinos all worked these fields, and the Japanese and the Chinese before that. From back when they were done with the railroads. The Chinese helped us get out of cattle and wheat, you know. And out of all of them, Mexicans are the best we've ever had. You do what we tell you, there's no talking back, and you don't ask for higher wages." He shrugged. "Sure, every once in a while we get wind of some strike talk, but that's just the work of outside agitators."

Tomás grinned. "A Mexican could never have a thought like that, right?"

"Hell no. You see, Mexicans are generally docile by nature. That's what makes them so perfect for this line of work. White men don't want these jobs. Even during the Depression, we had a hard time getting whites to do this work. And whenever we did"—Dallas chuckled as he took a few cards—"they quit so fast it made your head spin. I've seen them start in the morning, and be gone by lunch."

Tomás threw down a few cards and asked, "If nobody wants these jobs, then why are we hated for taking them?"

Dallas shrugged. "Just because somebody else don't want it, doesn't mean they're fine with you having it." He called and showed his cards. He won again. "Call it a grudge, call it the natural order of things, I don't know. But now that the war's over, and all the good jobs are in the cities, you're all we've got."

Tomás threw down his cards. "And vice versa."

Dallas nodded as Tomás collected the cards and shuffled. Dealing new cards, he asked, "Were you in the war?"

"Nah," Dallas said with a smile. "I was willing to go. Wanted to, even. Probably would have come back a hero, but my dad wrote me a letter and got me an exception on account of the ranch."

Tomás tossed down a card, took a replacement. "What do you mean?"

"I was deemed 'too important to the war effort.'" Dallas put down two cards, drew two others. "And it wasn't just me. Or our ranch. A lot of boys around here stayed home. We couldn't let anything interfere with business."

"Not even war?"

"Not even war." Dallas grinned. When he did, he looked even more like his dad. He called. Tomás beat him with a full house. He frowned while Tomás dealt again. As he was inspecting his cards, Dallas said, "How about you?"

"Me what?"

"Were you in the war?"

Tomás quickly fanned his cards, got rid of one of them, took another. "Yes, though it wasn't anything patriotic. When I was two weeks out of high school, my dad came to my room at five thirty in the morning. He handed me a black metal lunch pail and the classified ads. He said I had two weeks to find a job or else I would join him in the fields picking lemons. I joined the navy instead."

"How did he like that?"

Tomás grinned as Dallas got rid of a few cards and took new ones.

"Not too much. Because I was underage, he had to sign a form saying it was okay for me to go. When I brought it to him, he was wearing his khaki pants and undershirt, watching the news in his rocking chair, like he did every night. He was a bit shocked, but he signed it. After three months of boot camp in San Diego, I was supposed to have thirty days' leave. I was looking forward to being home for Christmas, but then the Japs hit Pearl Harbor and we shipped out to sea. It was years before I came home."

Outside, more men were turning in for the night. Doors of the other bunkhouses were opening and closing, the ancient bedsprings creaking and groaning. Snippets of conversations seeped through the paper-thin walls.

"Why'd you choose the navy?"

"Because I always liked the water. Needless to say, after my time on the ship, I don't like it much now."

"You see any action?"

"The ship did, I didn't. I was a machinist's mate, so I was always below deck." He called. Dallas won.

Tomás continued, looking over at Juanito, who had fallen asleep with the comic book on his chest. "I was on the USS *San Juan*. We provided artillery cover for the marines landing on Guadalcanal and Iwo Jima. I tell you, there's nothing louder in the world than war."

Dallas seemed impressed, but didn't say anything.

Tomás collected the cards and placed the stack in the middle of the table. "Well, it's getting late."

"Aw, and here I thought we were just getting started." Dallas leaned forward and said in a whisper, "I don't suppose you'd care to make things a bit more interesting."

"Meaning what?"

"Meaning we bet a little cash."

Tomás was about to say no, but as he sat up he felt Custodio's money in his pocket. He sat back down. "I shouldn't."

"I get it," Dallas said. "You know your limits. It's good to recognize when you're up against a better player."

"It's not that, believe me."

"Oh, I see. Well, I guess I was a fool to think a Mexican would have any spending money." Dallas spat on the floor and looked around the room. "If he did, why in the hell would he be here?"

A flash of anger burst across Tomás's face. He reached into his jeans and pulled out the money.

"Well, well, well," Dallas said, surprised. "What do we have here?"

Tomás peeled off a five-dollar bill and threw it on the table. Dallas got out his wallet and did the same. Tomás won the first hand, but Dallas won the next three. Two piles of cash quickly appeared, moving from man to man periodically. After half an hour, all the bills were sitting at Tomás's right elbow and Dallas was sweating under the light bulb.

He said, his voice raspy, "I have more up at the house."

Tomás looked out the window, but all he saw was black. "You do?"

"Yeah, a lot more. I'm good for it, believe me."

"Well, okay then. One more hand? Double or nothing?"

"Double or nothing." Dallas swallowed. "But I deal."

Tomás nodded. Dallas shuffled the cards more than was necessary and then dealt each one as if he were in slow motion. "Don't you peek," he said.

Tomás gathered his cards and kept them close together. Dallas splayed his out in a fan.

"And don't be hiding no cards neither. I got my eye on you."

There was no conversation as they played the final hand. Instead, they each looked to the cash and then back to their cards, as if for guidance. At one point, Tomás put his cards down on the table and wiped his brow.

After a few rounds of discarding and taking cards, Dallas said with a grin, "Call."

He went first, proudly putting down a full house. His arms were on their way to sweeping up the money when Tomás slowly, and theatrically, put down his own cards. An ace-high straight flush.

The smile that had been forming on Dallas's face quickly disappeared. "You greaser! You goddamned, no good lousy greaser!" He sat up in one quick movement, the chair shooting out behind him in a straight line. It hit Diaz's bunk and fell over. It startled Juanito, who woke in a daze. "You must have dropped your hand. There's no way you could have had that ace. I'd have known it."

Tomás didn't move.

"Speak, you lousy, cheating wetback!"

The men all came running when they heard the shouting. Santos led the way, with Claro and Custodio behind. They entered the bunkhouse, Custodio's crutch making a tunk-tunk-tunk sound as it hit the wooden floor.

At the appearance of the other men, Dallas looked worried and began to back up. He hit the wall and, thinking it was another person, turned around quickly to see who it was. He was face-to-face with the Virgin of Guadalupe. He grabbed one of the upper corners of the poster and tried to pull it down, but all he did was rip it in half.

Santos asked, "What's happening in here?"

"This greaser just tried to hustle me, but I ain't gonna let him." Dallas reached down and grabbed the pile of bills. He shoved them into his front pockets but quickly ran out of room, so he moved to his back pockets. "Damned Mexicans. I knew I shouldn't have trusted you. Once a wetback, always a wetback."

"You can't talk to me that way," Tomás said without much conviction.

"And why the hell not? I'll talk to you any goddamn way I please. I'm in charge and you're not. This is my ranch."

Tomás couldn't argue with that, so he tried something else. "Juanito, come here."

Juanito stood up. When he did, he created a shadow that covered Dallas.

"I just—I don't want no trouble," Dallas stammered.

Tomás said, quietly, "Get him."

Juanito didn't react, so Tomás turned and shouted. "Goddamnit, Juanito, I said to get him! This lousy liar's got our money!"

But Juanito just shook his head and sat back down on the bunk. The eyes of all the workers fell to the floor.

Dallas walked slowly to the door. No one made any move to stop him. He opened the door but paused and turned to Santos. The cool night breeze blew through the opening.

"Santos, I'm willing to forget this little incident. The fact that you allow gambling in the bunkhouses, not to mention that this man was cheating. But you need to keep the workers in line. You hear me?"

"Yes, Mr. Vaughn."

Before leaving the bunkhouse, Dallas took one last look around the room. No one looked up to meet his eyes. He grinned and left.

In the quiet that followed, Custodio finally spoke. "Was that my—"

But he didn't finish the question because he already knew the answer.

"Yes, Custodio, that was your money. I lost it, I'm sorry. I lost it all." Tomás threw his hand down onto the tabletop, striking the cards. As if it were all the cards' fault. "I had him, I tell you. I had him. The guy's just a lousy sport."

Juanito approached slowly. "He said you cheated."

When Tomás didn't answer, Santos asked the same question.

Tomás finally replied, staring at the ground, "Does it matter? They'll never let us win."

The other men walked to their beds and sat down. They took off their boots and jackets, preparing for sleep. One of them, seeing the ripped poster, made the sign of the cross. As they all settled into their beds, Tomás approached Custodio and whispered, "I'll get it back. Just you wait."

Custodio shook his head in an empty way. He didn't believe him. He didn't believe anything.

Tomás repeated, "I'll get it back, and more. Much more."

O N Saturday night, after working a half day in the fields, the men went into town. They packed themselves into rusty cars and headed to pool halls or dance halls or any cheap and comfortable place where they could nurse a beer for a few hours and swap stories of family or home. Those without transportation walked into Saticoy. Only a few stayed behind, writing letters to wives and children or to just rest and forget about the week about to end.

Without the conversations or even the hum of machinery and vehicles that usually ran around the clock, the ranch was quiet. Occasionally a car went by on the two-lane road outside the ranch, but otherwise all was silent. There wasn't even a breeze rustling the leaves of the lemon trees or the huge fronds of the palm trees that lined the driveway leading to the house where Vaughn, Dallas, and Celedonia lived.

Tomás, standing outside the empty dining hall—even the cooks and dishwashers had gone home for the night—looked around in the darkness.

Each of the buildings—the bunkhouses, the dining hall, and the packing shed—had a floodlight above its entrance, which only created a pool of light around each door. The ranch was not lit up in any other way, giving the grounds a ghostly sort of atmosphere.

He tried to orient himself in regard to the route he and Juanito had walked just the other day. He wondered if he'd be able to make it back to town when the sun was up, let alone at night. He always liked to know how to leave a place. It bothered him to be in the orchard without a clear idea of how to escape.

Suddenly, he heard a sound. A radio was switched on in the rancher's house. The music was tinny and filled with static, as if the signal was having trouble finding the meager antenna in the nearby mountains. Despite this, he could make out the tune and individual instruments. It was jazz. Tinkling piano, brushed drums, stand-up bass.

He followed the sound, walking to the beginning of the path behind the dining hall. He looked up at the big house. A window in the back was open. A patterned bit of green curtain wafted back and forth, the air inside moved by somebody. One light came on, and then another. In the newly created shadows he could see the holes made in the dirt by Vaughn's cane from the day before. No one walked on this path except him, and maybe Dallas when he was in a rush. Everyone else had to approach the grand house from the long driveway.

He went farther up the path. Overhanging cherry trees meant he couldn't see anything, not the lamps in the big house nor the floodlights from the ranch buildings behind him. It was so quiet and dark, it felt like a womb. He paused and just stood there. When he began walking again, it was slower than before. He was practically tiptoeing.

The path ended and the back porch of the house was in front of him. The music was now louder and clearer. He could make out the tune. "To Each His Own" by the Ink Spots. He'd picked almonds in the Central Valley the spring before last, and this song used to always be playing on the truck's radio when the workers were driven out to the fields. By the end of the season, he hated the song.

Stepping onto the first of four steps that led to the porch, he stood up straight and discovered he could see through the back window and into the kitchen. It was large, with huge white appliances and tall cabinets decorated with painted flowers and curlicue flourishes that reminded him of Dallas's shirt from the night before. There was a Formica and chrome table in the center of the room, with four chairs sitting around it. He figured this is where they ate breakfast and quick meals. Sandwiches for lunch, leftovers for supper. He wondered if the workers were ever part of their conversation, whether the people who lived here had any curiosity at all about the men who toiled in their orchards.

Tomás turned and looked toward the front of the house, to see if a car or truck was parked or was missing. But all he could see was more house. It was huge—three stories tall, the size of a small hotel. He marveled that only three people lived here. Surely they had some help. A girl to cook and do a little cleaning. Or maybe they had a whole staff, with butlers and maids in uniforms. A chauffeur to drive Vaughn to the bank and back, like Tomás had seen in movies.

When he took another step, the painted wood beneath his foot creaked slightly. There were two more steps, the porch, and then the back door. He wondered whether it was locked. He was betting that it wasn't.

He took another step, but this time there was a loud sound, as if the board under his boot was splitting and about to break. Tomás cursed the old house. He froze, letting the sound fade and seeing if it drew anyone to the back door or the window above. It didn't.

He was about to step again when a noise came from the road, a car backfiring. Another light came on in the house, this time on the first floor. He heard steps inside the kitchen. The porch became illuminated and Tomás cast a shadow.

He quickly descended the steps and retreated. The lights inside the house went out, and the path before him went dark once again. Trying to get back to the bunkhouse, he tripped over some exposed roots and fell.

Spitting dirt, he got up and began to run. He finally saw the light above the dining hall and headed toward it.

"Tomás?"

He looked up and saw Santos standing at the end of the dirt path. Santos's face was sweaty and his hands were covered in black grease.

"What happened to you?"

Tomás looked down and saw the dirt and dust on his jeans and shirt. "I fell."

"You fell," Santos said with suspicion, "or someone threw you down?"

Tomás, dusting himself off, looked up. "Do I look like the kind of guy people throw on the ground?"

Santos grinned. "Yes, actually. You do." He turned and started walking toward the bunkhouses.

Tomás followed him. "You didn't go into town with the rest of them?"

"No," Santos said over his shoulder. "I've been under that damn truck all night. Vaughn wanted me to make a couple of repairs, so I thought I'd just get it over with."

"Is he here? On the ranch, I mean." Tomás's voice was cool and casual, as if he didn't care about the answer.

"No, he and Dallas left this morning for a growers' association meeting in Fresno. They've been gone all day. Not sure if they're even coming home tonight."

Santos turned and examined Tomás. "Why aren't you with the others?"

Tomás looked at the ground. "I felt bad after what happened last night. Thought I'd give them all a bit of space from me."

As they turned the corner, approaching the row of bunkhouses, Santos said, "That was Custodio's money you lost, wasn't it?"

"How did you know?"

Santos smiled. "This is a small ranch, my friend. Whatever there is to know, I know."

"Yeah, well, then maybe you can tell me why that Dallas is such a lousy sport. And a cheat. I had him fair and square."

"Are you sure?"

As Santos was digging into one of his pockets, Tomás answered, "Yeah, I'm sure."

Santos stopped walking and held up a playing card. Two of clubs.

"It's a card," Tomás said. "So what?"

"I found it in the bunkhouse last night."

Tomás kicked at the ground. "Big deal. Small thing like that is bound to go missing. Why, when we first got here, those cards were scattered all over."

"I found this underneath the table. Wedged into the seam where the legs meet the top. Right where you were sitting."

"You saying I cheated? That I dropped a card like Dallas said?" Tomás's voice cracked slightly. "You taking his word over mine?"

Santos shrugged as a breeze blew past, carrying the sweet, grassy smell of the orchards. "I'm not saying anything." He handed the card to Tomás, who shoved it into his back pocket.

They approached the bunkhouse. Santos went inside and brought out two chairs. Tomás sat down while Santos went back inside. When he emerged, he was wiping his hands on a dark rag.

"They don't even give us a sink." Tomás spat on the ground. "Got to walk all the way to the dining hall just to take a piss or wash the dirt out of your hair. Lousy ranchers."

"You think this place is bad?" Santos laughed and motioned to the bunkhouse behind them. "This is nothing, my friend. A bit of peeling paint, a hard bed. Long hours. I've been at ranches where the men were served dog food. Or where they were kept in tin shacks in the summer and it was hotter inside than outside."

"It's not this particular place, I guess. It's the whole life I'm tired of. That's why me and Juanito are going to cut out of here the first chance we get and live some real lives."

"Ah yes. I heard about this."

Tomás stared at Santos hard. "From who?"

"Custodio. He came to me and asked what kind of man I thought you were."

"And what did you tell him?"

"I said you were a dreamer." Santos dug a pack of unfiltered Camels out of his shirt pocket. He fished out a cigarette, along with a matchstick that he lit with a flick of his thumb. He lit the short cigarette, inhaled, exhaled. "That's not necessarily a bad thing. You just need to be able to tell the difference between your dreams and what's real."

"Believe me, I know the difference."

"But do you? Just because you look at something, doesn't mean you believe that it's there. Or the other way around. A lot of men on the ranch are religious. They believe in all sorts of things they've never seen."

"Yeah, well, I've seen some things."

Santos nodded. "I've seen some things, too." He pointed to the darkened orchards with the glowing end of his cigarette. "You know, my family used to own land. Not far from here. Twenty thousand acres, a ranch bigger than this."

"Well," Tomás said, impatiently, "what happened to it?"

"It's gone."

"Gone?" Tomás asked. "What do you mean, gone?"

"Taken. Lost. Whatever you want to call it. And it wasn't just us. All the Californios lost their land."

"*Californios?* I don't know what that is."

Santos grinned. "Most people don't."

He dropped the cigarette to the ground and stamped it out with the heel of his boot. He got out a new one and lit it.

"The whole state was known then as Alta California. This was after the Spanish had been kicked out by the Mexicans, but before the Americans came in. Californios were the people who lived here. My family owned a grand ranch up near where Santa Barbara is now. But when the treaty of Guadalupe Hidalgo was signed in 1848, ending the Mexican-American War, that spelled the beginning of the end for us. The Americans were supposed to honor the deeds and the rights of the Californios, but almost immediately things went bad. Land challenges were just the start. That led to attorneys' fees and, finally, bankruptcy."

"Couldn't you fight it?"

"We tried, believe me. We'd owned the land for generations, but all we had to prove it were maps that showed trees, hills, rocks. The courts decided that wasn't good enough." Santos inhaled deeply. When he exhaled, the smoke created a crown around his head. "The case lasted for more than ten years, and in the end, the land went to the lawyers."

"What happened to your family?"

He shrugged. "What could they do? They had to

leave, get off their own land. Land that my grandfather and his father had farmed. They were given the option to work the fields, but only as tenants. As hired workers. That was too much for my grandfather, so they left."

"Where'd they go?"

"All over. They followed the crops from ranch to ranch. After they picked grapes up north, it was down to the Imperial Valley for work in planting and thinning lettuce, then oranges down south in Pomona, then back up to the grapes. By the time me and my siblings came along, even as a family, if we managed to pick two hundred boxes of grapes a day, we'd only earn seven or eight dollars. And that was with all of us in the fields. So we finally settled down in the Central Valley, not that it was much better."

"I grew up in Hollister, but I had cousins who were from out there. We heard some stories."

"I grew up in a ditch-bank camp, so I don't have to imagine what they were. Our house was a bit of canvas strung between two trees near an irrigation canal, underneath a couple of eucalyptus trees."

Santos finished the cigarette and immediately dug out another. He flung the lit match into the darkness, and as it flew, it looked like a shooting star.

"We got our drinking water from a well half a mile from the camp, or sometimes we'd walk to a gas station where they'd sell us water for five cents a bucket. We bathed and washed our clothes and our dishes in the canal. There was no sanitation, so there were flies everywhere."

Tomás laughed darkly. "Hollister's not looking so bad to me now."

Santos grinned. "When the Depression hit, things got even worse. My parents had both died, and two of my brothers went up to Oregon to look for work. There wasn't much to go around, and Mexicans were wanted even less than before, if you can imagine that. The local government thought we were getting too much of the little bit of relief being offered, that we were taking food out of the mouths of white people, so they started a repatriation program to try and get us to go back to Mexico. Even people like me, who'd never even been there. I was born here. I was an American citizen, but they were telling me to go back to Mexico. Well, I wasn't accepted in the States, so I thought I'd give it a try. They were offering free train fare to anywhere you wanted to go in Mexico, so we went. Me and a bunch of cousins. Of course, when we got there, the Mexicans didn't accept us because we spoke English. We couldn't win." He reached into his mouth and picked a bit of loose tobacco from his tongue. "We still can't."

"Was there at least work? In Mexico?"

Santos shook his head. "The country was still in ruins from the revolution. We discovered that everything they'd told us up here about life down there was a lie. Conditions were horrible, and we were unwanted in a country we didn't even know. At least in America we had gas ranges, but not there. Here we used flour for our tortillas, but there all we could get was corn. The women had to wake at four in the morning to make tortillas for the family, which we used instead of spoons. There was no running water, so we bathed in a small tub outside on the patio. It was almost as bad as my youth."

"So you came back."

"Yes, but it wasn't easy. When I first tried to return, I discovered they'd lied to us. They'd told anyone who left the United States that they could return anytime they wanted, but it wasn't true. They'd stamped 'LA County Charities' on the back of a card when I left, saying I had voluntarily left the country. I only later learned that this meant I could never come back. That, if I did, it would be a felony."

"So what did you do?"

Santos smiled and said, "I came back anyway."

"You came back illegally?"

"When you're hurting as badly as I was, my friend, borders are the last thing you think about."

"How did you do it?"

"I paid a border coyote $125 to take me across. We came over at night, me and a dozen others packed into a secret compartment in the back of a truck. An old man died on the way. It wasn't easy." Santos paused to take a drag from his cigarette. "When I got back here, I thought I'd try to get a little land. Maybe own a farm, like my father and his father. Only I discovered that that no longer exists. There are no small farms. All the best land is owned by just a few men."

Tomás looked around the ranch. "What about this place?"

Santos laughed. "This is only one of Vaughn's ranches. He has them up and down the state." He shook his head. "You don't know how powerful men like him are. The rules don't apply. They can do what they want, and usually do. And they only care about one thing. Money."

This time Santos stubbed out the cigarette against one of the legs of the chair. There were similar burn marks up and down the other legs.

"I had no idea he was so powerful."

"We tried to strike once. Vaughn didn't care. He sent word for more Mexicans, and the government supplied them. When we told the new workers about our struggles, a few came to our side, but not many. Then they recruited workers from Texas. They even got the local schools closed so they could use kids to work in the fields when we refused. We kept up the strike for almost a year. Finally, Vaughn broke it with thugs and criminals who beat us. Four men died and others were hurt so badly, they could never work again."

"What about the police?"

"Vaughn had the sheriff in his pocket, and they made deputies of everyone. Dallas was given a badge and a shotgun. I tell you, the growers' association has more power than the governor." He laughed darkly. "And all because people want to drink lemonade."

Something made a noise in the darkness. They both turned to look.

Celedonia emerged from out of the shadows on the dirt road, walking slowly with her head down and her arms crossed against her chest.

Santos's face turned into a grimace when he saw her, but Tomás grinned.

"Well, well, well," he said to himself under his breath, "what do we have here?"

She was wearing a black-and-white dress along with black high heels. Her lips and cheeks, covered with lipstick and rouge, practically glowed in the darkness. Her hair was pinned back, and hanging from her ears were earrings with some sort of glass or jewel that glinted in the moonlight.

"I hope we weren't keeping you up, Mrs. Vaughn." Santos rose from the chair. "Talking too loudly, I mean."

"Santos, you old fool." She waved his concern away. "It'll be a long time before I lose sleep over any of you."

The foreman stretched and faked a yawn. "I think I'll head in for the night." He opened the door of the bunkhouse, but before going in, bowed and said, "Nice to see you again, Mrs. Vaughn."

Celedonia shook her head as the door slammed shut, repeating, "That old fool."

Tomás grinned and examined her. "What can I do for you?"

"I have a question I'd like to ask you."

"I'm all ears."

"Dallas came home last night with a wad of bills. I want to know where it came from."

Tomás leaned back on the chair, tilting on its creaking legs. "I don't know what to tell you, darling. I don't know where Dallas gets his money."

"He gambles. He's told me so himself. There were some men here he used to play with, but they've moved on." She looked out at the orchards. "He was always coming home with cash. I felt horrible about it."

"Why?"

She turned back to him. Half her face was in shadows. "I was certain the men were letting him win."

"Now why would they go and do a thing like that?"

"Oh, don't be dumb. To stroke his ego. For special favors. Better duties in the fields."

"Losing to a man doesn't gain you his respect. In fact, it does quite the opposite." Tomás leaned forward, the front legs of the chair returning to the ground. "Maybe he just cheats."

"Dallas may be a lot of things, but he's not a cheat."

"Dallas, Dallas, Dallas." Tomás got up and kicked the chair. It scuttled across the packed dirt and fell over. "I'm tired of everyone sticking up for that guy." He turned and pointed to the bunkhouse. Santos's shadow could be seen on the wall. "You know how we're living down here? What our lives are like?"

She answered, no emotion in her voice and her face blank, "Yes, I know what your lives are like."

"Then maybe you could worry a whole hell of a lot more about us than about where Dallas gets his cash."

She approached him. "Was it your money that was lost?"

He turned. A car went by on the highway. It was late and the men would be returning soon. He just wanted to be alone with her. He glanced up to the house. "What if it was?"

She placed a hand on his shoulder. Her touch was light, like a bird landing on a branch. "Please tell me."

"Wasn't a lot." Tomás tried to sound casual. "I can always get more."

"Don't be foolish. For men like you, just a few dollars is a fortune."

Tomás grabbed her hand and flung it away. "Men like me? You think I'm the same as all the other Mexicans on this ranch?"

"Please, I didn't mean to make you angry."

Tomás took a few steps away from the bunkhouse. He hoped she'd follow him, but she didn't.

"Please, Tomás, don't."

Hearing her say his name did something to him. He turned around. The light from over the door was shining down directly on her. All he could make out on her face were those red lips. He walked back. "I'm sorry. I didn't mean to snap at you."

"It's okay. I know it's not an easy life." She looked down, her voice soft. "I actually didn't think you were the same as everyone else. I wouldn't have come if I did."

"I'm glad you did." He inhaled deeply, trying to get a whiff of her perfume, but all Tomás could smell was the fields.

"I know, but it's late—I should go."

"Celedonia, you just got here."

She looked up at the mention of her name. Another car went by on the highway. Men could be heard laughing and singing.

"I don't get to talk to many people on the ranch. Not in Spanish, anyway."

"Is there no one else up at the house?"

"There's a girl who cleans, but she's afraid of me." She motioned to the bunkhouse. "They all are."

Tomás gave his best sweet smile. "I'm not."

She reached up, grabbed a length of her hair, twirled it. "I know. That's why I like you."

Tomás took a step forward as Santos emerged from inside the bunkhouse.

"Mrs. Vaughn," he said, his voice deep, "I think it's time for you to leave."

Celedonia turned slowly to face him. "Mr. Velazquez, please don't tell me where I can and cannot go on this ranch." Her voice was stern and flat, like a teacher dealing with an unruly pupil. "You may be in charge of the men, but I can assure you, you are not in charge of me."

Santos shrunk in the doorway. "Sorry, ma'am," he whispered.

She cast a satisfied glance at Tomás and began to leave. As she walked slowly down the dirt road headed toward the big house, the movement of her hips caused the hem of her dress to sway back and forth.

He called out, his voice singsong, "Good night, Mrs. Vaughn."

She called back, over her shoulder, "Good night, Mr. Delgado."

As Tomás watched her turn the corner and disappear, Santos joined him outside the bunkhouse. "She's trouble, my friend."

"I know," replied Tomás, smiling. "And that's just the way I like them."

"I'm serious. If you fool with her, you won't know what you're getting yourself into."

"I'm not sure you ever do."

Santos shook his head and started walking toward the barn. "Follow me."

Tomás walked behind Santos, still grinning and trying to smell Celedonia's perfume and still failing. The barn smelled of manure and machinery. Turning the corner, he was hit with a new smell: rotten food. There were two large silver garbage cans. Santos raised the lids, tossed them aside, and kicked over the cans. The contents spilled out. Old newspapers, coffee grounds, eggshells, the bodies of the drowned dogs.

He grabbed Tomás by the shoulders and threw him onto the trash. He landed on one of the dead dogs. When he grabbed it to throw it aside, he could feel its muscles grown stiff under the still-wet fur.

"You want to end up like them?"

Getting up and wiping the bits of garbage from his shirt and pants, Tomás said, "I can only do what I can do. I don't know any other way to be."

"That's just more garbage. The choice is yours."

"I haven't had a choice in a long time. If I did, do you think I'd be here?"

Santos approached and looked like he was going to push him down again.

Tomás drew back and said, "You wouldn't be doing this if Juanito was here."

"What, your big friend?" Santos grinned. "He wasn't much help to you last night."

Tomás had nothing to say to this.

Santos continued, "And what if he doesn't come back at all? What if he's on his way to Los Angeles right now? Where will you go then? What will you do?"

"Juanito's nothing without me. He couldn't even wipe his nose."

Santos threw his head back. "He's smarter than you suspect. Most people are, I think. If they weren't, why would we be here? You think you're smarter than Vaughn and Dallas, and yet they live in that big house and you don't."

Tomás, stomping his way back to the bunkhouse, snapped, "Yeah, well, we'll see about that."

Turning the corner, headlights raked the trees. Cars were turning off the highway. Three of them pulled in and let out a dozen men. Most of the men were drunk; some were half-asleep and being helped by another. Custodio and Juanito got out of the last car. Custodio was limping a bit, but no longer needed his crutch. Juanito walked in his usual way, pigeon-toed and with his face tucked into his chest, eyes looking at the ground.

Santos called out, "You boys have a good night?"

Custodio smiled and pointed to Juanito. "I did, but this one sure is a puzzle. I took him to the movies, but he spent most of the film in the lobby watching the popcorn machine."

Juanito raised his head slightly, but didn't make eye contact with anyone. He said, simply, "I like popcorn."

The cars turned around and headed back to the road, a few of the men waving to the drivers and thanking them for the ride. They honked and, in a second, were gone.

As the men began to file into the bunkhouses, Santos called out to Claro. "How were the others?"

Claro looked up. His eyes were red, and he was weaving slightly. "It was a good night. I saw only a few fights. One bracero, from the labor camp, was sent to the hospital with a knife wound."

"As soon as he's healthy," Santos said, "they'll send him back to Mexico."

Tomás held Custodio back as the others entered the bunkhouse. "You still want to come with us? Go to Los Angeles, I mean?"

Custodio's eyes went wide. "Yes, of course. More than anything."

"And you'll be ready to go as soon as I say? Maybe even tomorrow?"

"I could leave right now if we had to." Custodio pointed to his bed through the open door of the bunkhouse. "There's nothing here that I care about. Say the word, and I'll go."

"Okay, good," Tomás said.

Inside the bunkhouse, the men were settling in for the

night. One or two of them were already asleep, passed out in their clothes.

"Just watch for my signal, okay?"

"Okay," said Custodio. "But how? Where will you get the money?"

"Don't you worry about that," Tomás replied. He looked up to the rancher's house. One light, on the second story, could be seen through the trees. "I have a plan."

T HE BASEBALL GAME was in its seventh inning. The
sun was high in the sky, and a breeze kept the workers cool as they played. The team at bat was trailing by
two runs.

The teams, which had been quickly chosen after lunch,
were unnamed and informal. A few of the men who'd
been on the ranch a long time were regulars, having
staked out their respective positions long ago, but the
rest of the lineup varied depending on who was working
in the orchards that week. There was no manager, no
scoreboard. Some players didn't even have gloves. No one
placed bets on who would win. The men did it just for
fun.

They played in a field on the other side of the packing
shed, the diamond crudely cut into the dirt by bootheels.
The distance from home plate to first base was not quite
equal to the distance between either first base to second,
second to third, or third to home, but no one com-
plained. The bases themselves were fashioned out of anything the men could find. First base was a trash-can lid,

second and third bases were men's jackets held in place with stones, and home base was a flattened cardboard box. The lid from a crate of lemons served as the pitcher's mound. Chairs had been carried over from the dining hall and set up at the bottom of the diamond, and those who weren't playing, or who hadn't walked into town, watched and cheered the game.

Santos, sitting between Custodio and Juanito, leaned over and spoke into Juanito's ear. "We started these games last year. It's a nice thing to do on a Sunday afternoon. A lot of the ranches do it. Down in Orange County the growers sponsor a whole league, and over in Fillmore, a ranch has a small stadium." He laughed. "A few of the men from the old country tried to organize cockfights, but I persuaded them that this would be better."

As a player approached the makeshift home plate, he spat on his palms and rubbed them together before picking up the pine bat. Tall and lean, he was one of the few men to wear sneakers. The rest of them were wearing work boots. The batter let two pitches go by before slapping a ball right through the legs of the shortstop. He flung the bat aside and took off running, quickly rounding first base and then second.

"Wow, that guy's good," Custodio said as the man slid into third base.

"That's Gonzalez," said Santos. "Played for the Oxnard

Aces back in the thirties. If he wasn't a Mexican, he would have gone to the Majors."

The next batter swung at and connected to the first pitch. The ball arced high in the sky and began to fall toward center field. Diaz, in the outfield, walked slowly and carefully to catch it, shielding his eyes from the sun. When the ball finally landed in Diaz's glove, Gonzalez scrambled back to third base and the hitter, halfway to first, turned around.

Santos again addressed Juanito. "Do you like baseball?"

At first, Juanito didn't reply. When he finally raised his head, his squinted eyes were no more than slits cut across the huge slab of his face. He said no, quietly.

The next batter approached. He had strong arms and broad shoulders. When the pitcher saw him, he turned and waved the center fielders into deeper territory. The man swung wildly at the first two pitches, grunting as the bat turned into a blond blur in his powerful hands. The pitcher grinned, thinking he was getting the better of him. After the pitcher delivered two balls into the dirt, the man swung at a fastball. He connected and the ball shot through the air like a rocket. Everyone followed with their eyes as it sailed over the field. The ball finally fell out of the sky and landed on top of the packing shed as the men broke into applause.

Tomás, inside the packing shed and startled by the sound, sat up quickly.

He'd been in there for twenty minutes, his heart only recently beginning to beat at its usual pace. But the noise on the roof, along with the cheers of the men outside, made his pulse race once again.

The enormous structure was a maze of chutes, conveyor belts, and stations where the fruit was sorted, graded, and packed. Along one wall, hundreds of empty crates were stacked up to the rafters. The square ends of the boxes had colorful labels that read GLORIOUS BRAND CITRUS. The picture below the words showed a Spanish Mission surrounded by palm trees set amid orange and lemon groves. In the distance were mountains framed by a blue sky and mustard-yellow sun. Below the picture was printed *Albertson Lemon Association* and underneath and even smaller was *Saticoy, Ventura County, California.*

Tomás was sitting on one of the conveyor belts that led to a huge tub, where the fruit was bathed in chlorine and wax. The tub was empty now, the steel a dull gray in the half-light.

In front of Tomás was a large pile of cash. Ones, fives, tens, and even twenties. It was more money than he'd ever seen in his entire life. His legs were crossed and his elbows were on his knees, his chin resting on curled fists. On his face was a huge smile. Tomás stared at the money, as if he were a child and it was telling him a story.

He leaned down and inhaled deeply, trying to get a whiff of the cash. But all he could smell was the packing shed's strong odor of lemon oil and bleach. He made a face.

"I can't wait to get far, far away from this goddamn place." He reached into the wad of bills and ran his fingers around the various curves and folds of the paper. "I wonder where I'll go? Up north, maybe. Or back east."

He leaned back, laying down flat on the belt. He looked up to the rafters of the packing shed. Lamps were hung every twenty feet or so, and above the stack of crates was a clock. It was almost five.

"Dinner," he said with disdain. He kicked at the gray rubber of the conveyor belt. "I wonder what slop those fools are going to eat tonight?"

He rolled over and pulled the money close to him. He made a pile of it next to his chest, pawing and stroking the bills just like Custodio had petted his puppy earlier in the week. He began to count it, but quickly lost interest. It was a lot, and that's all that mattered.

There was a noise behind him, but he just took it to be part of the game that was still going on outside.

"Hello? Tomás?"

He froze. It was Celedonia. He quickly pushed all the

money into the tub. When the conveyor belt was free of the cash, Tomás sat up and turned around.

"Why, hello there." He tried to sound suave, but there was an edge in his voice.

She was wearing a red wrap dress with lapels like a man's blazer and a neckline that created a deep V. Around her neck she wore a string of pearls. They glowed against her brown skin. A black beret sat on the back of her head and around her waist was a large black belt made of felt with a big bow on the front, as if she were a gift wrapped up just for him.

"I've been looking for you," Celedonia said.

"Well, it looks like you found me."

She walked toward him, slowly. "Wait a second," Celedonia said, "how'd you get in here?"

Tomás nodded toward the door. "You think they lock it?" He looked around the huge space. "Nothing in here worth stealing." Tomás hopped down off the conveyor belt. He walked around her in a circle. Her hands were clasped behind her back, and one of her wrists held a chunky bracelet with a dozen dangling charms. One was a cable car, another a crescent moon.

"Do you make it a habit to steal things?"

"Only women's hearts," he replied.

She blushed and looked away. There was noise outside, the men cheering. "Why aren't you out with the others, enjoying the game?"

He noticed that her voice had a flutter to it. She was nervous around him. He liked that. "Baseball's not really my sport."

"What is your sport?"

He considered this as he examined her shapely legs. Her stockings had a dark line down the back of them. "I don't really like sports, now that I think about it."

"How about your friend?"

"Juanito?" Tomás hadn't thought of him all day. "He doesn't like anything that has people in it."

She looked down at the ground. "I don't believe you."

"It's true. Now, if you gave him some big mechanical toy, one that had little tinmen hitting a ball and running around little metal bases, you wouldn't be able to tear him away from it. But real-life flesh and blood?" Tomás shook his head. "Juanito couldn't care less."

"Then why are you traveling together?"

He grinned. "I don't know how much longer that's going to last."

"You get a better offer?"

"Something like that."

She took her eyes off Tomás and scanned the room. He watched her examine the various corners of the packing shed. He couldn't tell if it made her happy or sad. He asked, "How long has it been since you've been back here?"

Celedonia walked around and looked at the various

stations. She ran a finger up and down one of the machines. "I come here from time to time. Chat with the girls. See how they're all doing."

"You still know any of them?"

"You mean, from when I worked here?"

"Yeah."

She shrugged. "Those girls have mostly moved on."

"To better things, or just to other ranches?"

"I don't know where they went. I don't know where anyone goes when they leave here. I just know that they go."

"Well, people like us, we don't have too many options." Tomás grunted. "We leave a lot, but we always end up at the same place."

She turned around to face him. "Maybe you need to keep trying." She made it sound like a command and not a suggestion. "Work harder, and stop looking for a hand-out."

"Sister, don't you talk to me about work. I've been working my whole life."

"I have, too."

"Not anymore, you don't." He spotted a lemon on the floor and picked it up. It was perfect. Lightly dimpled, tapering a bit toward each end, no blemishes. He threw it the length of the shed. It dropped without a sound. "Not since you met Dallas, anyway."

She didn't respond. Instead, she walked toward one of

the packing stations. The wooden stands where the crates sat at an angle at the end of the conveyor belt were all empty. Tomorrow there would be dozens of women manning these stations, the whole room a riot of noise and activity.

"Tell me," he said snidely, his voice echoing off the tin walls, "why did he notice you?"

"What do you mean?"

"Dallas. Out of all the other girls, why you?"

Celedonia grinned and blushed. "I don't know . . . you'd have to ask him."

"You sure you didn't seduce him?"

Something happened in the game outside. There were gasps followed by applause.

"I don't know what you mean."

"Oh, come on. He was your ticket to a better life. That was certainly worth a batted eyelash and a short skirt or two."

She turned quickly and faced him. "You really are a nasty little man, aren't you?"

"You live up in that big fancy house with your rich husband. What the hell do you have to worry about anymore?"

"Tomás, don't be like that."

"Don't tell me what to be like. You don't know me."

"Oh, yes I do."

"You told me that yesterday."

She was about to speak, but stopped. She breathed deeply. "You know, last night—I saw you."

"I saw you, too," Tomás said. "We had a nice chat, remember?"

"No, before that." She moved a little closer and softened her tone. "That was you, right? On the back porch?"

His face exploded into a smile. He looked at the ground, at the ceiling, at the huge machines all over the room, anywhere but at her.

"Maybe it was."

She smiled, too.

"I thought so. It was like, I felt you. Out there. Down there. Looking up at me." She edged closer to Tomás. "Did you want to come in?"

"Yes, I did."

"Then why didn't you?"

"I just—I didn't know who was home."

She was now just inches from him. "Would it have mattered?"

"Maybe. Maybe not." He could finally smell her perfume. Rose petals. It just about killed him.

"I was home, Tomás. Just me. Alone."

He put his arms around her and pulled her close. She struggled slightly at first, as if she knew it was a bad idea. But when he kissed her, she softened. Her shoulders, which had initially risen in protest, fell. In their embrace they leaned into the conveyor belt where Tomás had been sitting when she entered.

He moved to her neck, pulling her hair lightly and kissing behind her ear.

"The men," she mildly protested, "they're right outside."

"I know." He continued to plant kisses on her lips and neck. "They'll be out there having a good time, and we'll be in here having a good time."

She smiled and turned her head so he could kiss behind her other ear. "Money," she said.

"What?" He tried to kiss her again to keep her from speaking or opening her eyes, but she pulled away and pointed to the bottom of the tub.

"There, money. A lot of it."

"Never mind that. Kiss me."

This time she roughly pushed him away. She looked back and forth, from the money to Tomás, from Tomás to the money, as if trying to figure out where either of them had come from. She finally said, in a whisper, "The house."

She backed away from him. "The house," she repeated. "You stole that from our house, didn't you?"

"Not your house, Celedonia, their house. Those goddamn greedy ranchers."

He reached out for her wrist, but she pulled it away. "Dallas is my husband."

"That didn't seem to bother you a minute ago."

"That's different."

"Different how? Look," he said, trying to soften his voice, "it's just the money I lost off him the other night. The way I look at it, I didn't take anything that wasn't mine."

She looked again into the tub. "You couldn't have lost that much to him. Not in one night."

"Well, maybe I did take a little more."

"But why?"

"Teach Dallas a lesson."

"If you wanted to teach him a lesson, you'd stick around and show him you're a good man. You'd earn his respect. You wouldn't steal from him and then run off like a coward."

Tomás grinned. "What makes you think I'm planning to run?"

"Isn't that what you all do?" She shook her head and said, more to herself than to him, "Probably been running your whole life."

"Goddamnit, lady, I'm not about to hear another lecture from you."

There was silence for a moment. There was no sound from the baseball game outside, and Tomás and Celedonia just stood there.

"Last night," she said, as if suddenly remembering. "You didn't want me, you wanted the money."

He was going to protest, but no excuse came to mind.

"That's why you were skulking around outside the house. It had nothing to do with me."

"Come on, baby. Don't be like that."

He reached out and again pulled her close to him, but she balled up her fists and beat his chest. "You bastard," she said, her voice filling with anger. "You rotten, lousy thief!" She hit him harder and called him names, her voice getting louder and louder. He tried to put a hand over her mouth to keep her quiet, but she kept wriggling out of his grasp and raining down blows on his shoulders and face. He finally, in an act of desperation, picked her up and threw her in the tub with the money. She landed with a dull thud.

"Wait until I tell my husband," she gasped. Gripping the sides of the steel tub, she gathered up more breath and began to pull herself up. "Wait until I tell Vaughn. You'll never work on another ranch in this state."

Tomás glared at her and began to walk off. He was storming out of the packing shed when he saw the tools. Scattered on top of a long workbench near where they made the crates were crowbars, saws, hammers. Next to a number of half-finished crates was a stack of GLORI-OUS BRAND CITRUS labels. He stopped for a second, looking over the bench. Behind him, Celedonia was pulling herself out of the tub.

Tomás grabbed a crowbar, raised it over his head, and

ran toward her. She had time to look up, but not to make a noise. He swung the crowbar sideways, connecting with her head just above her left ear. Her head jerked violently, blood came out of her right ear, and she fell backward into the tub. Her pearls, as she landed, hit against the bottom of the tub and made a metallic clank.

Breathing heavily, Tomás dropped the crowbar. From where he was standing, he couldn't see into the tub. The money and Celedonia were both out of sight. It was as if neither existed and he could just walk outside and join the others.

Taking a step forward, he saw one of her feet and part of a leg. Taking another step he saw the hem of her dress, as well as some of the money.

He rushed to the tub and began to frantically reach down and pull out the cash. Some of it had blood on it, and some was already warm from Celedonia's body being pressed against it. He tried not to look at her, but he had to know where to grab for the bills. Her mouth and eyes were open, and her head was twisted away from the body, as if it'd come off and been reattached in the wrong spot. He grabbed the last of the cash and walked back to the bench of tools.

He took one of the labels and placed it on the bench. He quickly arranged the money into a stack and folded the label around it. He tucked the parcel under his arm, looked around, and exited the packing shed.

The baseball game was just ending in a round of cheers, Gonzalez being led off the field on the shoulders of his team for hitting the winning run. As the men made their way to the dining hall, talking about the game and recounting various plays, Santos noticed that the door to the packing shed was open. He broke off from the rest of the men and stepped inside.

"Hello?" He walked into the huge building and looked around. He repeated, "Hello? Is anyone in here?"

He saw the crowbar on the ground near the conveyor belt. As he walked toward it, thinking that some worker had left it there the day before, he saw a shoe. And then a leg. He paused briefly before continuing. Then he saw the whole body. And the blood.

"Sweet Jesus."

He ran back to the door and called out to Claro, who was just entering the dining hall with Diaz, Custodio, and Juanito.

"Get Dallas down here," he shouted. "And maybe even Vaughn, if he's there. We've got trouble."

Claro nodded and ran up the dirt path to the house as Santos retreated back into the packing shed. Diaz, curious, approached the building. Custodio followed with Juanito behind him, his head down and knocking his knuckles together.

When the men appeared at the door, Santos looked up and frowned. "Go away, please. You shouldn't be here."

But they didn't listen. The trio approached, slowly, not sure what they were going to find. When they saw it was Celedonia, and that she was dead, nobody said anything. Nobody knew what to say.

Outside the packing shed, there were voices. Dallas speaking English and sounding upset.

"I'm a busy man, Claro," he was saying as he entered the building. "I don't have time to run all over the god-damn—"

He ceased speaking when he saw the others. The men parted to let him approach. Dallas looked from face to face. He spotted the crowbar on the ground. None of this made any sense. He stepped forward. When he saw Cele-donia, he froze.

"Why?" he muttered, his face falling. "Why?"

His hands gripped the sides of the tub so hard his knuckles turned white. "Sweetheart," he whispered. "No."

Suddenly, as if snapping out of a trance, he barked at the men, "Well, don't just stand there, gawking. Get her out of there!"

Santos yelled at them in Spanish to remove her from the tub. Claro and Diaz stepped forward, and they, along with Santos—grabbing and lifting her by the shoulders, waist, and legs—pulled her out. Custodio and Juanito stood by, watching.

They laid her out on the conveyor belt. As they did so, one of her shoes came off. Through the stockings there were toes painted red to match the dress. Dallas approached and tried to set her head in the right direction, but it just wouldn't go. Dark purple blood began to pool on the gray rubber of the conveyor belt. A second later, it spilled onto the floor, making black dots on the gray concrete. Dallas tried to close her eyes like he'd seen done in movies, by simply brushing his palm from her forehead to the tip of her nose, but it didn't work. He removed Celedonia's beret and placed it over where her face was frozen in a ghoulish stare.

He said, slowly, "Did anybody see who did this?"

"I discovered the body, sir," Santos said, stepping forward. "But I didn't see anything. None of us did. We were all on the other side of the packing shed watching the game."

"Everybody?"

"Well, not everyone. Some of the men went into town. And a few others were—"

Dallas interrupted. "What about the big guy's friend?" He pointed to Juanito. "The one I beat in poker the other night. Was he at the game?"

"Tomás?" Santos considered it. "I haven't seen him since this morning. I don't know where he is now."

Dallas turned from Santos back to Celedonia. "He did this, all right. He wanted to get back at me. Well, I guess he did."

No one knew what to do next, not even Dallas. He

finally said, "I'm going to go after him myself. I have a shotgun up at the house. He's not going to get away with it."

"Dallas, please," said Santos. "You don't need to do that. Surely the police will pick him up. He doesn't have a car or any money. He won't get far."

"Yes, he will."

"But how?"

"Because he's also a thief."

"Sir?"

Dallas's face reddened. "I came across it an hour ago, after my dad and I got home from up north. I keep cash in a drawer in my dresser. For emergencies or spending money. For the last half hour I'd been talking to the girl who cleans the house, trying to get her to admit she took it. But, after this, I'm sure it was your friend." He motioned to Celedonia's lifeless body. "She must have caught him in the act and followed him down here. He killed her just to keep her quiet, the coward."

Santos nodded. It seemed possible. He'd heard worse stories, seen worse things.

"I'll go up to the main house and call the sheriff in Ventura. Give him a description. The lousy bastard's probably out on the highway right now trying to hitch a ride." Dallas was speaking normally now. He was used to being in charge and giving orders, and his wife's murder was just another thing to manage on the ranch. "I'll go into Santa Paula and see if he's dumb enough to head there to get a bus somewhere. Or maybe he headed to Saticoy. Either way, I'm going to find him. He's not going to get away with this."

There was noise from outside, the first wave of workers exiting the dining hall.

"Santos," Dallas said, "let the rest of them go and eat, but you're coming with me."

Santos was about to protest, but knew it was pointless. He said, meekly, "Yes, sir. But only if you promise you'll try and take him alive."

"Alive?" gasped Dallas, his voice rising. He pointed to his dead wife. "After what he did to her? He'll be lucky if I don't shoot him in the stomach and let him bleed to death right there in the street, the lousy greaser."

As they were all filing out—Dallas in the lead—Claro pointed at the body.

"Dallas," Santos called out. "What about . . . her?"

Dallas, suddenly remembering, turned back around. "Yes, thank you." His voice was soft again. Seeing her did that to him, not that it'd ever do that to him again. "I'll get the girl from the house to come down and stay with her until the ambulance comes. She'd want to be with one of her own kind."

Santos nodded.

Dallas approached the body and stroked where a cheek was exposed by the beret covering her face. He turned, but then stopped. He picked up her left wrist and took off the charm bracelet. He shoved it deep into his pocket. After standing silently for a few seconds, the men all staring at the ground, Dallas turned. "Until we catch him," he sounded stern again, "none of you tell nobody nothing about what you saw, you hear?"

Dallas realized they couldn't understand what he said, so he turned to Santos. "You tell them to keep their mouths shut."

Santos told the men in Spanish to not tell anyone what they'd seen. They all nodded and left the packing shed.

As Dallas walked up to the house with his head hung low, Santos went to get the truck, and Claro and Diaz headed toward the dining hall. Juanito was about to follow when Custodio pulled him away and guided him to the other side of the large tin building. The baseball diamond could still be seen in the dirt, and home plate was still there, but the other bases and the pitcher's mound had been swept away in the excitement of the game's ending.

"Juanito, I need you to think." Custodio was whispering even though no one was around. Across the ranch he heard Santos starting up the truck. "Do you know where Tomás is headed?"

"Tomás? Where's Tomás?"

"I don't know, Juanito. That's what I'm asking you.

He's done something wrong. Something bad. Do you know where he is?"

"Baseball game," Juanito said quietly. "I remember the baseball game."

"Yes, Juanito, but this is something else." He grabbed Juanito by the arms and shook him, trying to get the huge man to look into his eyes. "Tomás is in trouble. Serious trouble. We need to find him before Dallas does."

Juanito finally looked up. "Tomás? Bad?" His whole body slumped and his head fell. "Not again."

"Yes, Juanito, and we need to find him or else they're going to kill him. Do you know where he might have gone?"

"Los Angeles," he said, quietly.

"You think he's headed to Los Angeles?"

"I want to go to Los Angeles. My uncle's expecting me. I should have been there weeks ago. Los Angeles."

Custodio was getting angry, but he tried not to let it show. He repeated, calmly, "Tomás, Juanito. Your friend, Tomás. Do you know where he is?"

Juanito just shook his head. Custodio decided to try something else. "Where were you before you came to the ranch?"

Juanito looked up. "Before we were here?"

"Yes, Juanito. Before you came here, just the other day. Where did you come from? Maybe that's where he'll go back to."

Juanito thought. "Hollister. No, that's where we started from. Lettuce. Goleta. That's where we were. But then we had to leave."

"Yes, Juanito, that's good. Keep going."

His eyes opened. They were big and brown, with almost no white. "The river. We spent the night at the river."

"In Saticoy?"

"Yes, Saticoy. Right across from town."

He grabbed Juanito's hand, and together they began to walk toward the two-lane road. There was still dust in the air from the truck leaving, heading for Santa Paula.

Custodio said to Juanito, "We just might have a chance."

Tomás kept looking over his shoulder as he jogged along the main road, keeping an eye out for the police or the truck from the ranch. Once or twice a car passed by, and when it did—just to be safe—he darted into the fields and hid among the trees. He was sure that by now Celedonia's body had been discovered, or the money had been found missing, and either offense would send Dallas and Vaughn after him. He figured his best bet was to get to town and hide out by the river until it got dark. Once night fell, he could approach a stranger in one of the bars and pay them a few dollars to take him far away in any direction.

As he tried to make his way back to Saticoy, he searched in vain for landmarks he might recognize from the other day. But everything looked maddeningly the same. Palm trees, eucalyptus trees, lemon trees. It was an endless maze of orchards and fields, and none of it looked familiar.

Finally, after turning down a dead-end road, getting disoriented, and heading back the way he'd already traveled, he saw Saticoy off in the distance. But he quickly discovered that, as he got closer to town, he began to lose the cover of the trees. It was just him and the road, with nowhere to hide.

Clutching the money tightly to his chest, he sprinted the last hundred yards, running across the road and skipping into the brush by the river like a jackrabbit.

He found the clearing where he and Juanito had spent the night. The brown paper bag that had held their meager dinner was still lodged in a bush, crumpled into a greasy ball. Seeing it reminded him that he hadn't eaten since breakfast. His stomach began to growl.

Tomás looked up. He had at least an hour before the sun dipped below the horizon, and he'd need at least another hour after that for it to be dark enough for him to emerge. Food was still a long way away.

He kicked at the sandy bank of the river before sitting down. "Once I get out of here, I'll have more food than I can eat."

He put down the money and picked up a handful of sand, letting it run through his fingers. "And good food, too. Not like that garbage they served back at the ranch."

He wondered what the men were doing at that moment. He tried to picture them in the bunkhouse later that night, after the news had got out. He was curious about what they would say or think. Then he shrugged. "I've done what I've done. There's no changing it now."

He thought of Juanito, but pushed the image of him out of his mind as soon as it entered.

Looking down at his hands, Tomás noticed they were sprayed with blood. Tiny specks of dark purple that looked like freckles. He thought of Celedonia, but pushed her out of his mind, too.

Tomás got up, kneeled by the water's edge, and plunged in his hands. The river was ice-cold. Once his hands were clean, he made a cup out of a hand and took a few sips. He was hot after running from the ranch, so he splashed handfuls of water against his face.

As the cool water dripped off his head, he got a look at himself in the river. His unkempt hair was hanging down, and his face looked long and tired, like how he remembered his father always looking.

He sat down and thought of his dad. It was March, which meant his father's birthday was coming up soon. Just a few weeks. Tomás tried to think of what today was, but couldn't. The sixteenth? The seventeenth? The exact date escaped him. He tried to think back to when he last saw a calendar, but nothing came to mind. Maybe Goleta. Maybe before then. He looked down at his wrist, but he hadn't owned a watch in years. He'd had a nice one, when he was in the navy, but he lost it in a card game in San Francisco the first weekend he was back.

Tomás picked up a few pebbles and slung them into the water. He couldn't get any of the pebbles to skip more than two times. He thought again of his father. He pictured him in his khaki pants, undershirt, work boots. His face had been lined with creases, even though he died young, at fifty-one. Tomás thought of the piercing eyes, cleft chin, and the rough gray mustache that divided his face in two. His voice was deep and strong. Tomás's voice was a poor imitation.

He took the bundle of money from under his arm. The parcel was warm from being held tightly against his body. "I know I've made some mistakes, but I'll make you proud, Dad. You'll see."

He peeled back the label so that he could get a look at the bills. He finally counted them up. It wasn't quite as much as he'd thought. It'd hold him for a couple of months, half a year if he stretched it. But he'd have to get another job eventually. Would once again have to pick grapes or lettuce, oranges or lemons. He thought back to the walk he'd just taken from the ranch to the river, how the orchards seemed like a maze. He was beginning to think it was a maze he'd never find his way out of.

Behind him, something moved. He turned his head quickly, but it was just a lizard scurrying underneath some dried brush. From Saticoy he could hear a car's horn, along with the sound of men's voices. The bars would soon be filling up. He looked again to the sky. It was already beginning to turn pink. It would soon be purple and then finally black. That's when he could leave this place for good.

He turned back to the river. Mountains loomed above trees, and in the sky, a flock of crows circled and harassed a hawk. Tomás heard another sound behind him, but thought it was just the lizard again. Then he heard a voice.

"Tomás."

He stuck the money underneath his arm and jumped up. "Juanito," Tomás said with a fake smile. "I'm so happy to see you. You alone?"

Juanito walked a few steps instead of answering. He kicked at the sand, looked at the river, and then back to where Tomás was shifting his weight nervously from foot to foot. When he finally spoke, it was so quiet Tomás had to lean forward to hear the whispered words. "You left me."

"Aw, Juanito, don't say that. I didn't."

"Yes, you did, Tomás." Juanito was staring at the ground. "You were going to leave me there. At that ranch."

"I was going to come back for you, honest. As soon as night fell. I was going right back there to get you."

Juanito took a deep breath and shook his huge head from side to side. "That's a lie, Tomás. You were never going to—"

"Look, Juanito, be quiet." Tomás stepped forward and produced the parcel of money. He showed some of the cash. "We can go to your uncle's. All we need to do is get a ride into Oxnard. We can grab a bus from there and be in Los Angeles by midnight."

Juanito looked down at the money, puzzled.

"The plan," Tomás continued. "To stop running. To belong. We can do it, Juanito. You and me. Today."

Juanito pointed at the cash. "Where did you get that, Tomás?"

"That's not important, Juanito." Through the trees, Tomás could see Custodio limping along the sidewalk outside of a small market. "What's important is that I have it. It's mine. I mean, ours. And we can leave this place. Tonight."

"If you have money, why can't we leave right now? Let's just get in a car and go."

"I just—it's complicated, Juanito. People are looking for me."

"What people? Who?"

"Dallas and Vaughn. People from the ranch. And maybe the police."

Juanito suddenly remembered. "The girl, Tomás. You hurt that girl."

"That's a lie. I didn't hurt anybody. Not on purpose, anyway."

"I saw her, Tomás. There was blood. It was bad."

"It was an accident, that's all. Just an accident."

"But she's dead, Tomás."

He shrugged. "Bad accident."

"And that money." Juanito pointed again. "You took the money, didn't you?"

Tomás shook his head, as if trying to shake off Juanito's questions. "Do you want to pick lemons for the rest of your life, or do you want to get out of here?"

"Stealing wasn't part of the plan, Tomás."

"I know, Juanito, but sometimes plans go wrong. This is our chance to make it go our way for a change. For once. Don't you want that?"

Juanito looked away from Tomás. He glanced over his shoulder, toward where he and Custodio had walked from the ranch. "You need to go back."

Tomás took the package from under his arm and stuffed it into his shirt. "I told you, I'm not going back."

"What you did was wrong."

"Goddamnit, Juanito—when you got nothing, nothing is wrong." Tomás began to pace up and down the riverbank.

"You need to go back," Juanito repeated. "Stop running. That's what you said."

"They're going to kill me," Tomás said, panic beginning to edge into his voice. "Don't you see that?"

"You'll go away," Juanito replied without emotion. "It won't be so bad."

"Wise up, you damn idiot." Tomás's voice was now

shaking. "Those ranchers will shoot me if they find me. I'd see never see a trial, much less a jail cell."

"You need to come back to the ranch. With me and Custodio. Maybe it won't be so bad."

"I'm not going back to that ranch, Juanito. The bunkhouse is just another kind of jail cell, and I'm tired of it."

"I don't understand any of that, Tómas. I just know what you did was wrong."

"Yeah, well, running back to that goddamn ranch certainly isn't going to make it right."

Juanito stared at the ground instead of answering.

Tómas continued to pace back and forth, only now he was in a frenzy. His heels kicked up clumps of sand as he made circles on the riverbank. He finally came to a stop and said, slowly, "There's no way out of this, is there?"

Juanito just flapped his arms a few times.

"No way out," Tomás repeated. "No way out."

Out on the road, a car stopped. Tomás heard doors opening and closing, and then voices. He craned his neck and saw Dallas and Santos talking to Custodio. Dallas was carrying a shotgun, and Custodio was pointing to where Tomás and Juanito were standing. Dallas and Santos began to cross the road.

"You have to do it. Right now."

"Do what?"

"Kill me."

"What?"

"It's the only way. Please."

"No, Tomás. I've never killed anything. I don't want to kill you."

"You have to, Juanito. If you don't, they will." Tomás pointed to where Dallas and Santos were making their way through the bushes and trees, heading toward the river. "And I'd rather the last face I saw be a friendly one. Please, Juanito. Do this one last thing for me, and then you'll be free. I won't get you into any more trouble."

Juanito looked up, finally interested. "No more trouble?"

"No more trouble."

"Then I can go to my uncle's?"

"Yes, Juanito. Then you can go to your uncle's."

"You promise?"

"I promise."

Juanito looked as if he was going to take a step forward, to approach Tomás, but he didn't. "I can't, Tomás. I just can't." He began crying. It was the first time Tomás had ever seen him cry. "Please don't make me do this." He wailed like a child. "Please, Tomás. No."

Ignoring his pleas, Tomás took the large man's hands from where his arms were dangling at his side. He tried to fasten them around his neck, but Juanito's grip was soft and slack. He refused to squeeze.

"You big idiot, do it!" screamed Tomás.

But Juanito just continued to stand there, sobbing.

Tomás nudged him over to the river. They both waded into the water.

"Tomás, it's cold."

"You're not here for a swim, goddamnit. Drown me." He pointed to the water. "Kneel, Juanito, hurry."

Juanito did as he was told, and even though the water was icy, his face showed no emotion or reaction.

"Over there!" A voice, behind them. Dallas. "I can see them!"

Tomás sat down in the water. It was deeper than he thought, and his head went briefly under. His whole body shook from the cold. The river was also running faster than he remembered from the other day. The current began to whisk him downstream. Eddies and swirls began to form around them, creating waves and bubbles. He had to hold on to rocks to keep from being swept away.

"Do it, Juanito. You'll be doing me a favor."

But Juanito was still crying, and his hands on Tomás were only to push him away, not to keep him under.

"Juanito, do this one thing and you can go to your uncle's."

Tomás looked up and saw something on Juanito's face. A grim recognition. The tears stopped. Tomás finally felt the strong hands grip his shoulders, and he was violently plunged under the water's surface.

He opened his eyes, but all he could see were rocks

and gray light shining through the water. Out of instinct, his hands found the bottom of the river and he pushed himself up. He gasped desperately for breath. He heard Juanito say, "Stop running," before he was plunged under again. He swallowed mouthfuls of the river. As he fought against Juanito's grip, he felt his strength beginning to leave him. He could almost watch it disappear.

Being underwater made the noise above muffled and sound far away. He thought he heard voices, someone shouting. Then a loud noise that sounded like a fire-cracker. He held on to Juanito's wrists so tightly that his nails dug into the flesh, but still he was held under.

Tomás thrashed, and swallowed more water. His head was slammed against the rocky bottom. A cut on his fore-head bled into the river and made the water purple and cloudy. He changed his mind, but by then it was too late.

When the body finally stopped moving, Juanito let go. Tomás became just another bit of debris floating downstream.

"Jesus Christ," Dallas said, standing at the foot of the clearing. Two trails of smoke floated out from the barrels of his shotgun. Juanito hadn't reacted when Dallas called out to him to stop, nor had he reacted when Dallas fired into the air.

Juanito was still kneeling in the water, his empty hands hovering above the surface.

"Stop running," he repeated. "Stop."

As Dallas dropped the shotgun to his side, Custodio and Santos caught up with him. They all stood at the outer edge of the riverbank, looking upon the scene.

Juanito stood up. His clothes were drenched. Tomás's corpse had floated just a few feet before getting hung up on some branches. Juanito, his head down and his face expressionless, walked out of the water and up onto the shore. Santos moved toward where Tomás was floating, but Dallas stopped him.

"Leave him, Santos. He's right where he belongs."

Juanito, his clothes dripping water onto the sand, approached the men but kept on walking, heading toward town. They watched him pass.

Dallas was turning, to head back to the truck, when he saw a few bills surface from underneath Tomás's bloody body. Then more appeared, as if Tomás was a piñata filled with cash that had burst. The bills turned in the waves and floated downstream.

"My money!" Dallas shouted. He ran to the water, but then stopped and turned around. "Goddamnit, Santos, get in here and help me."

Dallas plunged into the water and began slapping at the surface, grabbing the bills before they floated away. Santos reluctantly joined him, half-heartedly reaching for a bill here and there while Dallas turned Tomás over and rifled through the dead man's pockets before wading downriver to grab the rest.

Custodio turned and followed the path back to town. Limping out to the road, he found Juanito standing on the sidewalk. His clothes, as he stood in the sun, were already beginning to dry. "Let's just go," Custodio said, quickly. "Before they come back."

"Go where?" Juanito asked, not looking up.

"To your uncle's. To Los Angeles. Do you have the address?"

Juanito nodded, but added, "I don't have any money."

"We'll figure out a way."

"How? I told you, I don't have any money."

"We'll walk if we have to." Custodio shot a look toward where Dallas's truck was parked down the street. "I'm not going back to that ranch. You shouldn't either."

Juanito raised his head slightly and opened his eyes. "I don't like that ranch."

"Then let's go. You and me. Now."

Juanito focused on Custodio for a second before lowering his head yet again to the ground. "Okay," he said, softly. "Let's go."

Custodio smiled and hobbled into traffic, trying to wave down a car. One or two slowed down, but ultimately swerved to avoid him. Finally, a yellow pickup stopped. Custodio pointed to Juanito, told the driver they were heading to Los Angeles, and asked if they could both be given a ride. The driver, dressed in work clothes, smiled and waved them inside. He offered to take them as far as Calabasas.

Juanito shuffled slowly across the road while Custodio limped to the passenger side and got in. He left the door open. Juanito joined them, barely fitting. Custodio reached across him and shut the door. The driver put the truck into gear, pulled away from the curb, and drove out of Saticoy.